KILL THE HUNTER

BRYAN SMITH

Grindhouse Press
PO BOX 540
Yellow Springs, Ohio 45387

Grindhouse Press #097
ISBN-13: 978-1-957504-11-7

This one is for my youngest brother, Eric Smith, a great person who deserves all the happiness in the world.

ONE

THE MAN WITH THE EYE patch was holding a gun to his sister's head when Zach Murphy walked into the kitchen.

This was shortly after he'd gotten home that afternoon. An annoyingly talkative Uber driver who hailed from Texas had dropped him off in the street outside less than a minute earlier. The man's rambling diatribe about Longhorn football and the apparently unquestionable superiority of Texas BBQ over BBQ from anywhere else had made him wish he had a screwdriver handy so he could puncture his eardrums.

It wasn't the content of what the man was saying that bothered him, though none of it was anything he cared about. What annoyed him was the man's loud, boisterous, fast-talking manner of speech. It grated on his nerves and left no room for interjection, not that he actually cared to participate in a conversation with the rowdy Texan.

At that point, as he exited the vehicle, he was blissfully unaware of the violent chaos that would soon engulf his life. Later on, he would sometimes reflect on those last few moments of existing in ignorance of the dangerous threats that lurked in so many of the world's darker corners. He could see himself mounting the steps to the front porch that day, just a kid not long out of high school. An innocent in so many ways.

KILL THE HUNTER

A kid who was about to learn that some of the mythical things that go bump in the night are real.

TWO

ZACH CAME TO A DEAD stop in the kitchen, a fleeting wish to still be in the back of the Texan's late model Mustang flitting through his mind. The desire was shameful and understandable at the same time. On the one hand, any sane person, upon unexpectedly encountering an armed and scary-looking, one-eyed stranger in their place of residence, would likely experience an instant desire to be anywhere else. This was a normal human impulse. The feeling of shame stemmed from knowing that not being here in this moment—or until after the man was gone from the house—would condemn his sister to being alone with a murderous psychopath.

Zach had no actual knowledge yet of the intruder's intentions or motive for being here, but he figured murderous psychopath was an unfortunately safe assumption. This was an intruder who'd violated the sanctity of their home. He had a gun pressed to Chelsea's head. What looked like an old knife scar trailed down one side of his face, from the corner of his one remaining eye down to the tip of his chin. The scar was a thick ridge of swollen flesh, suggesting a deep slice by a blade of significant heft. He perceived a demented aspect to that one ice-blue eye, which seemed to pulse in its socket. The man was tall-ish, around six feet, and possessed an intimidating physique, with huge muscles straining the fabric of a black shirt.

Zach was familiar with the old saying about not judging a book by its cover, but in this case he felt perfectly justified in doing so.

This guy was a psychopath, no doubt about it.

Zach froze in place and felt his guts curdle as the man took the gun away from Chelsea's head and pointed it at him. His mouth was hanging open and he had a thumb hooked under one of the straps of his backpack, in preparation of removing it. His impression of a statue ended the instant he saw the muzzle of the man's weapon aimed straight at his face.

His knees started to shake.

Then his whole body was trembling.

The man's voice was surprisingly soft when he spoke, with an almost feminine quality to it. "I'm going to ask you a question, Zach Murphy. If you don't answer truthfully, you and your sister will suffer. Do you understand?"

Zach did not understand.

He couldn't imagine what information the one-eyed man thought he possessed that would warrant such threatening behavior. This was all so mysterious. He was a normal kid who didn't do bad things or run with a rough crowd. He'd never harmed anyone and was pretty sure the same was true of Chelsea, who was still in high school.

His entire family was respectable and unassuming. They did okay, but they weren't rich and there was nothing of any great value in their home beyond ordinary things like semi-expensive electronics. There was no secret fortune stashed away in a safe. No rare art masterpieces were hanging from the walls. He had a couple of semi-rare comic books that might fetch around fifty bucks on eBay, but that was about it. Nothing a man like this would be after.

He couldn't make the slightest lick of sense out of what was happening.

But he made himself nod and stammer out an answer. "Wh-what . . . do you want?"

The one-eyed man sneered. "I need to know where Jonathan Murphy is."

4

THREE

THE MAN'S WORDS PROMPTED A groan from Zach. The disfigured psycho was looking for their estranged father, because of course he was. He wasn't aware of his dad being up to any shady business, at least not prior to abandoning his family a year earlier. As for what the man might be up to these days, he knew almost nothing, and judging from the look the one-eyed man was giving him, he was not going to be happy to hear that.

An understatement of gargantuan proportions. The man was tightly wound, on edge, and ready to explode. His teeth were clenched tight, one side of his mouth twitching and quivering. In Zach's opinion, he lacked the calm, even-handed disposition anyone handling a firearm should possess.

Instead of answering right away, Zach studied the look on his sister's face. She did not appear to have been harmed. He saw no evidence of welts or bruises, which came as a huge relief. Just the concept of this brute laying his big, meaty hands on his sweet sister with the intention of hurting her made him sick. Their mother sometimes referred to Chelsea as a "slip of a girl", meaning she was small, slender, and barely an inch above five feet. A man like this psycho could snap her in half as easily as anyone else could break a pretzel.

Zach made eye contact with Chelsea.

She was terrified.

Tears streamed down her face. Seated in a chair pulled slightly away from the big, round dining table, she looked pale and shaky, her mouth moving in a way that reminded him of the time she'd become violently ill on a family trip to Florida a few years back, not long after eating at a Cracker Barrel. He'd been sitting in the backseat of the SUV with her when she abruptly groaned and lurched forward, clutching at her stomach. She'd turned her face toward Zach and shown him an expression that was a mirror image of the one he was seeing now. Seconds later, she was screaming at their father to pull over to the side of the road, which he promptly did. Then she was out the door and on the shoulder of the road, commencing a round of projectile vomiting that rivaled that of the possessed girl in *The Exorcist*.

The one-eyed man gestured with the gun. "Did you hear me, boy? I know you're not deaf, so I'm pretty sure you did. You better start talking if you want to make it out of this alive. I'll shoot her in the fucking head if you don't tell me what I need to know right now. Swear to God I will."

Chelsea's grimace of pain stabbed at Zach's heart. A length of her long dark hair was wound around the man's other hand, had been the whole time, but Zach was only now realizing it. What had changed was that the one-eyed man was now pulling hard at it, perhaps hard enough to feel like it was on the verge of being ripped out of her scalp. Her head tilted backward to a sharp degree, but not far enough she couldn't make eye contact with her brother. She still hadn't said anything, but those eyes were pleading with him, begging her older sibling to save her somehow.

Zach's expression hardened. "You're hurting her."

The one-eyed man laughed. "This is nothing, boy. It's just a taste of what's to come if you don't tell me where I can find Jonathan Murphy."

Chelsea started blubbering, weak cries that soon gave way to louder sobs and moans. She was still looking at him in that desperately pleading way. He couldn't fault her for her distress. In her place, he'd be just as scared. He was plenty scared already, but he knew his terror would be off the charts if he was the one sitting in that chair. Pants-pissing scared. The maddening thing was Chelsea knew he didn't possess the information the man wanted.

There was nothing Zach could do in terms of physical

intervention. All he could do was to stall and obfuscate, maybe buy enough time to allow some miracle solution to present itself. This felt super important. Say he told this man the truth, that he rarely talked to his dad and had no idea where he was. It was difficult to imagine a man this on edge walking out of here happy without the information he was after. Conversely, it was extremely *easy* to picture him shooting them both in the head before departing.

Zach realized he'd been holding his breath and now he slowly released it. "Why are you so desperate to find my dad? I mean, we're not real happy with him these days after ditching us the way he did, but he's a pretty ordinary guy, straitlaced and boring. Honestly, he's too nerdy to be involved with anything that would get him in trouble with . . . well, with someone like you. You sure you don't have him mixed up with someone else?"

The one-eyed man smirked. It was his first expression of anything resembling humor. "You're describing a false version of your father, an illusion he created. He kept things hidden from all of you. Things that would disturb and sicken you if you knew any of it. He's dangerous. A threat to anyone who crosses his path."

Zach made a scoffing sound and shook his head. "Bullshit. That's ridiculous."

The one-eyed man's smirk disappeared, his expression turning grim. "I'm afraid it isn't. And you're stalling." He shoved the muzzle of the gun against Chelsea's head, making her squeal. "You've got about ten seconds to tell me what I want to know. If you don't, I'll fire a hollow point round into your sister's head, pureeing her brains. It'll be messy and ugly and it'll be all your fault. This is your last chance to save her."

Zach's pulse quickened as he began to panic. He felt close to hyperventilating. The circuits in his brain felt like they were misfiring continuously, the right pacifying words—the ones that might save his sister's life—eluding him.

The one-eyed man began a countdown. "Ten, nine, eight . . ."

He was speaking fast instead of dragging it out. His index finger was inside the trigger guard, squeezing against the trigger. One more tiny degree of pressure against it would bring a devastating result. Chelsea whimpered helplessly. She spoke for the first time since Zach's arrival, repeatedly saying his name in a tremulous voice filled with despair.

". . . four, three, two . . ."

7

Zach said, "I don't know where my father is. I swear to God that's the absolute truth. Please don't hurt my sister."

The one-eyed man glared at him for a moment.

Then he took the gun away from Chelsea's head and pointed it in Zach's general direction.

A loud boom filled the kitchen.

FOUR

THE EARDRUM-PUNISHING CONCUSSIVE NOISE was the report of a firearm discharged in close quarters. Zach had never fired a weapon of any kind, but he knew that sound, having often heard it in video footage of mass shootings shown on the news. He was also familiar with the sound of gunfire from countless movies and TV shows, but that was the Hollywood world of make-believe, with sound manipulated to deliver a particular effect for the audience. The real thing couldn't be mistaken for anything else.

That he'd heard it at all was Zach's first clue he'd not been shot in the head. Had that happened, he likely would have perished immediately, hurled into the darkness of a void from which he could never return. The impression was augmented by the sight of the big man flinching as a bullet struck him high on the shoulder, a bright red spurt of blood leaping from the exit wound.

Despite being shot, the one-eyed man remained on his feet and leaned over Chelsea as he attempted to adjust his aim and return fire. In the same instant, a hand clamped on Zach's shoulder from behind and moved him aside. He turned his head and gaped in astonishment as his mother moved fully into the kitchen, a snub-nosed revolver clutched tight in her upraised right hand. The sight of the woman who'd birthed him into the world wielding a gun blew his mind so thoroughly it temporarily flushed it clean of anything resembling coherent thought.

He'd never seen his mom with a gun before, had never even known she owned one. Noreen Murphy had spent the bulk of her adult life as a full-time mom. She spent a lot of time engaged in activities like volunteering at the local animal shelter and participating in fundraisers. Typical small town housewife stuff. She was demure and ladylike and Zach never in a million years would have imagined her capable of violence, nor of the elite level of ninja-like stealth that was apparently also a part of her particular set of skills. There was no truly quiet way of entering their house that he knew of, yet she had managed it.

Before more shooting could ensue, Chelsea grabbed hold of the one-eyed man's arm and clamped her teeth down on the bulging underside of his muscular forearm. He'd left himself open to this mode of attack by leaning over her, making the mistake of thinking the undersized girl he'd been menacing was not a threat. He screeched in pain and tried jerking his arm away, but Chelsea held on with the tenacity of a rabid bulldog. She managed to keep her teeth firmly embedded in his flesh even as he swung her about like a ragdoll, her thrashing body knocking over the chair she'd been sitting in moments ago. Blood welled up around her mouth and flowed freely out of the wound as she snarled and shook her head frenziedly, shredding the flesh.

Once again, Zach was flabbergasted.

The one-eyed man stumbled away from the table until his back met the French doors that opened onto the small deck out back. Chelsea fell away from him and hit the floor. The man looked dazed for a moment but stepped forward and began to raise his gun again. Before he could squeeze off a round, Noreen Murphy shot him again, this time in the head. A spray of blood painted a stripe of bright red across one of the French door windows. The man's gun flew from his hand and clattered across kitchen tiles as he collapsed to the floor.

Rather than taking a moment to breathe a sigh of relief or check on the well-being of her kids, Noreen was in motion again almost immediately. The one-eyed man's gun had come to rest in front of the refrigerator. She scooped it up and hurried back across the kitchen, thrusting the weapon into the hands of her only son, who gaped at it as if she'd just given him a bomb with a lit fuse.

Then he looked at his mom and said, "Wha . . ."

He trailed off because he didn't know what else to say. His brain was still short-circuiting. Too much had happened in too short a time. Violent, bloody things that made him feel like he'd stepped out of his ordinary life and into a movie or some alternate reality. His mother was saying something, but at first he couldn't decipher the words, it was like he was hearing them from underwater. Then she grabbed him by the shoulder and gave him a hard shake.

"Zach!"

He blinked and let out a breath. "What?"

At least this time he'd managed to enunciate the entire word. A miniscule amount of progress but better than nothing.

She snapped her fingers in front of his face. "Are you with me? I know you've had a shock, but I need you to be one-hundred percent present and focused. This isn't over. Do you hear me?"

A second or two of silence, just long enough for Zach's brain to finish recalibrating.

Then he nodded and said, "I hear you. I'm here. I'm listening."

The slightest twitch of a smile briefly touched the corners of his mother's mouth, there and gone so fast it was hard to know whether it'd been real or illusion. "I need you to put that man's gun in your backpack. The safety's on now. It's that switch right there." She indicated it with a stab of her index finger. "If you need to shoot somebody, push it down with your thumb."

Zach squinted. "Shoot somebody?"

Her expression turned grim. "Yes, Zach. I told you this isn't over. Or at least there's a good chance it isn't. There's a lot I don't know yet myself, and I don't have time to explain the things I do know."

Zach glanced at the one-eyed man's unmoving form. He was seated on his ass in a slumped position, his back partially against the French door. His head was lolling to one side, his mouth hanging slack with a thin trail of drool at one corner. Blood seeped from a wound creasing the left side of his head. It hit him that the man was not yet dead, a realization that led to a renewed sense of encroaching panic. He looked like maybe he was unconscious, but even that was hard to know with any certainty. That the bullet hadn't punched through his forehead instead of digging a shallow groove through the side of his noggin came as a slight disappointment. He was in no way eager to see splattered brains, but it would've finished the man as a threat in a more definitive way.

Noreen snapped her fingers near his head again. "Zach!"

He looked at her. "I don't understand. Why don't we just call the police? Hell, somebody must have heard the shots. They're probably already on the way."

Noreen grimaced. "Yes. And that's why we have to move fast. Do like I fucking told you and put the gun in your backpack."

Zach did a double-take. He couldn't help it. It was the first time hearing his prim and proper mother use any form of the f-word in his eighteen and a half years of life. The word itself didn't offend him. It was just jarring hearing it out of his mother's mouth. A number of deeply held illusions were being shattered here, one after another at a rapid clip.

He caught a glimpse of his sister opening the refrigerator and removing a bottle of Yoo-hoo. She screwed off the cap and drank from it. There was no evidence of the terror or shakiness of mere minutes ago. If not for her face being covered in the one-eyed man's blood, you'd think nothing of an upsetting nature had occurred.

Zach made eye contact with his mother. "I just don't get it. Why are we worried about the police? We've done nothing wrong. That man broke into our house. He threatened to kill us. You'll probably get a fucking medal for shooting him."

Noreen slapped him.

Not hard enough to hurt, but a slap nonetheless. An attention-getter.

"Whoa. Mom, what the hell?"

"You're still not focusing. And watch your mouth. Don't go throwing around f-bombs just because you heard it from me."

Zach thought they probably had much bigger things to worry about than his use of profanity, but he accepted what his mother was saying with a nod. "Okay."

She grabbed him by an arm and started pulling him through the archway leading out of the kitchen and toward the front of the house. The bottom line was this was his mother. She'd always stood up for him and protected him. He had no reason not to trust her, even under the most messed up circumstances.

They arrived in the foyer.

Noreen opened the front door but paused before pulling it fully open. She plucked the gun from Zach's hands and made him turn around. After opening his backpack, she slipped the gun inside and zipped it shut again. Then she opened the door and stepped out onto the porch, tugging Zach along with her. Chelsea followed right on their heels, bottle of Yoo-hoo still in hand.

Zach scanned the area outside the house and saw no sign of his mother's Pathfinder SUV. Not in the driveway and not at the edge of the lawn where she sometimes parked when she was in a hurry. If they were fleeing the scene for some inexplicable reason, he didn't see how they could get very far without a vehicle. His old Celica was at an auto body shop, undergoing some repairs. It was why he was getting around via Uber for a few days. Chelsea didn't have a vehicle of her own yet, though she did have a driver's license.

Maybe he should order an Uber again?

No, it would take too long.

He didn't have to think about it much longer because, within seconds of stepping out onto the porch, Noreen was pushing something else into his hand. His brow furrowed when he saw her keys pressed into his palm. "What am I supposed to do with this? I don't even see your car."

She closed his hand around the keys. "It's parked three houses up the street toward Sunny Day Lane. Take your sister and go now. Get on the interstate and don't stop driving until you reach Lakemoor. Stop at a gas station there and send me a text. I'll call you right back and tell you more, but for now you need to go."

Zach huffed in exasperation. "You're freaking me out, Mom. Why should we do that? I don't understand."

Noreen groaned. "And there isn't time to make you understand. I promise I'll tell you everything when I can." She gave him a push toward the edge of the porch. There was an even more intense fierceness to the cast of her features now. She looked like a woman on the edge, dangerous and desperate, capable of anything. It was scary. "Go, Zach. Now."

She went back into the house and shut the door.

Then came the unmistakable sound of the door latch clicking shut.

Zach shook his head in disbelief.

Turning around, he saw Chelsea already walking across the lawn, moving at an angle that would take her in the direction of Sunny Day Lane. Muttering a curse, Zach took off after her.

He didn't know what else to do.

FIVE

THE ONE-EYED MAN WAS stirring as Noreen returned to the kitchen. His eye looked bleary as he pushed away from the French door with a groan and sat up straight. He touched the shaky tip of a finger against the wound at the side of his head and winced.

Noreen picked up the fallen chair and turned it so it was facing the man who'd terrorized her children, careful to place it out of sudden kicking or lunging range. She sat down and pointed the Ruger LCR at his face.

He looked at her, grimacing as he again lightly touched the side of his head. "You can kill me, it doesn't matter. They'll just send someone else. And someone else after that. Until they get what they want."

"Meaning my husband."

He shrugged, wincing again. "Would go easier for everyone if you just say where he is. You and your kids don't need to be involved. Just give him up."

She ignored that and asked him, "How did you get onto him? Given the many layers of protection involved, it shouldn't be possible."

The one-eyed man chuckled and tried sitting up a little straighter, stopping when he gasped in sudden pain. "No one's so well hidden they can't eventually be found. And fuck you for shooting me. Your husband is dangerous. He needs to be found. I'm only doing my job, trying to protect innocent people."

"My children are innocent people. They're just kids. What you were doing was vile."

"I did what was necessary. This is an urgent situation. I'm tracking a monster. They might have known something."

Noreen shook her head. "They know nothing. That's the truth. I have no reason to mislead you now. They're clueless. And you terrorized them. Brutalized my little daughter."

The one-eyed man sighed. "Okay, I believe you. Now. But how was I to know that? People hiding big secrets tend not to tell the truth unless you scare them."

The next several seconds ticked by in silence as Noreen studied his face, which was shiny with sweat. Blood was still seeping from the wound at the side of his head and from the one to his shoulder. The wounds were more than merely superficial, but they were not life-threatening. That was by design. Any normal person would see that head wound and assume she'd missed the mark, that she'd been trying to kill him, but that was not the case. She'd wanted him alive so she could interrogate him.

"You still haven't told me how they got onto him after all this time. Bear in mind I will know if you lie. And if you lie, I won't bother threatening you. I'll just shoot you in the kneecap. So tell me what happened."

The one-eyed man glared at her. "I'd love to shove that little pop-gun up your ass." He sneered, looking her over. "Along with something else."

Noreen nodded. "I'm sure that's true. So much for your phony benevolence." She moved a hand, adjusting her aim. "Let's forget about your kneecap for now. Answer my question or I'll shoot you in the dick. You know I'm not playing."

His leering sneer remained in place a moment longer. Then he shrugged. "Some information came to light a few days ago."

"How?"

An amused smile replaced the sneer. "You're right, you know. We probably never would've known, except that your husband placed his trust in the wrong person."

"Who?"

"His best friend."

Noreen's expression turned skeptical. "Bullshit."

There was only one person not married to him who could accurately be described as Jonathan Murphy's best friend. His name was Elliot Valentine. They'd known each other almost as long as she and Jonathan had been living in this town, a span that encompassed nearly two decades. They were more than just friends. Some men maintained male friendships only on a surface level, but these men were confidantes. They knew one another inside and out. Elliot was that one person anyone would wish to have on their side in a crisis, the friend who'd help you bury a body if necessary and take the secret to their grave. Noreen would have bet her life on it being an unbreakable bond, impervious to betrayal.

She would not, could not believe what this loathsome man was saying.

The one-eyed man sneered again. "Not bullshit. His name's Elliot, right? Elliot Valentine?"

Noreen got a cold feeling deep inside upon hearing the man say the name. She tried to keep her face impassive and not show him anything, but within seconds she knew it was pointless. The man had seen her expression change the moment he'd uttered the name. Just a quick flicker lasting no more than a fraction of a second, but it was enough.

The man smiled. "Yeah. See? I know things. I'm not just some hired goon with a gun. I'm a professional, a man working an assignment. Nothing more, nothing less. I have no reason to bullshit you. Elliot Valentine gave up your husband for two reasons. Cold, hard cash, for one thing. Our standard reward for tips leading to the elimination of creatures like your husband. The second reason is that he's in love with you."

Noreen laughed. "Elliot Valentine is in love with me? You can't be serious."

"But I am. He . . ." The one-eyed man's head wobbled slightly as he trailed off, his body listing to one side for a few seconds before he abruptly righted himself and shook his head. "My head is swimming. I'm losing too much blood. I need medical attention."

"I'll consider doing something about that after you finish what you were saying. Not one second sooner."

The man coughed and cleared his throat. "He's been in love with you all along, from even before you were married. Man's been playing the long game, waiting for something to come along and drive a wedge between you and your husband, but all these years went by and it never happened. He got frustrated, then even more so after Jonathan disappeared. He thought he'd finally get his chance, but you didn't let him get close enough because you were holding out hope your man might return. Elliot finally realized the only way he'd ever have a real chance with you would be Jonathan's death."

Noreen's eyes narrowed as she attempted to process this bewildering information. "At which point he'd presumably swoop in and sweep me off my feet?"

The one-eyed man shrugged. "That was his hope anyway."

Noreen laughed. "That's insane. He told you all this?"

He shook his head. "Not me directly. My boss conducted an interview. A thorough one. It's necessary with allegations of this nature. Proof has to be offered. Elliot provided it in spades. All this stuff I just told you? It's all in your husband's file."

Noreen believed him.

She hated to admit it, but she had a finely tuned sense of when she was being deliberately misled and that was not the case here. That mild tingling sensation she got at the base of her skull when someone was spewing lies was not present. Acknowledging this made her feel betrayed and sad. Elliot had been her friend too. She hadn't picked up on his potential for duplicity because she'd trusted him without question, something she didn't know if she'd be capable of ever again.

The one-eyed man watched her carefully as she silently processed this information. Now he said, "You believe me. I see it in your eyes."

Noreen nodded.

She stood up and moved the chair out of the way. The would-be assassin's eye tracked her as she moved, a deep wariness visible in every twitch of his increasingly pale features. She set the gun on the table and kicked off her high heels.

He looked afraid and was starting to shiver.

"If I don't get your husband, someone else will. The next guy they send will be worse than me. I know who they send in on the difficult cases, when the first guy doesn't come back. He's a different kind of monster altogether. They call him the Annihilator. You should cooperate while you still have the chance. Save yourself and your kids. Jonathan Murphy isn't worth it."

Noreen removed the belt from her waist and draped it over the back of another chair. She pulled her dress off over her head and draped it over the same chair. A frown creased her features. She dragged this second chair away from the table and set it close to the archway. Satisfied with its placement, she removed her underwear and dropped the garments on the seat of the chair.

She heard the man's strained grunts before she turned toward him again, and guessed what he was up to before seeing it. When she saw him, he was swaying on his knees, his hand shaking like a leaf as he leaned over the table and reached for the gun.

Noreen smiled. "Still hoping to shove that up my ass?"

The one-eyed man said nothing and continued straining for the gun, which was well out of his reach in his debilitated condition.

Noreen approached him and shoved him back to the floor, where he landed with a heavy thump and moaned in misery. She stood over him and smiled again as she felt her exposed nipples stiffen. "It's been far too long since I did this."

He stared up at her, blinking in confusion. "What do you mean?"

She laughed. "You don't know as much as you think. Your bosses don't either, apparently. You see, there's more than one monster in this family, more than one daywalker, and you're looking at her."

The one-eyed man let out a cry of fright as she opened her mouth wide, baring her newly elongated fangs.

The cry gave way to a short-lived scream of terror as she fell atop him and clamped her mouth against his throat. A primal thrill of exhilaration flooded her system as she drove her fangs into his flesh and began to greedily slurp up his blood. He thrashed beneath her and tried punching the side of her head, but nothing worked. She was too strong, her dormant vampiric abilities awakening at the taste of fresh, hot blood. She held him beneath her easily, enjoying the way he struggled as well as the convulsions that followed. This was an indulgence she hadn't allowed herself in years, taking blood from a live human being rather than in prepackaged form. It was delicious. It was *divine*. Every drop felt like a taste of heaven. No drug on earth could match the sensation. She continued to drink deeply from him until he stopped moving and beyond.

Until he was gone.

Until he was empty.

SIX

"YOU'RE GOING TOO FAST."

His sister's words took some moments to penetrate. She'd said nothing at all up to now, a stark contrast to the manic yammering he'd engaged in as soon as they were ensconced in the SUV. She'd stared straight ahead the entire time, gazing through the windshield with a blank expression as he drove them out of the neighborhood and out to the interstate. Every few minutes she raised the bottle of Yoo-hoo to her lips and took a small sip. There was something robotic in these occasional small movements, an impression of disconnection.

Zach continued talking for several minutes straight without interruption before realizing Chelsea wasn't absorbing even the smallest bit of what he was saying. By that point his hyped-up stream-of-consciousness articulation of extreme worry and confusion was beginning to run out of steam anyway. He transitioned to peppering her with a rapid-fire series of questions about the bizarre events they'd just experienced. What did she think was behind all of it? What could possibly explain why that scary bastard was so desperate to find their father? Why had their mother been so cryptic in her comments before sending them away?

Why, why, fucking *why*?

Again, she failed to respond to any of it.

He gave up and allowed his thoughts to turn inward as he attempted, without success, to puzzle out explanations on his own. Despite joining his sister in silence, his state of agitation failed to decrease by even an iota. He felt like the world was spinning out of control and there was nothing he could do to stop it. Given the circumstances, the separation from their mother was terrifying. They had no clue yet what had happened to her following their departure. Had the cops showed up and arrested her for shooting that guy? Or, even worse, had the man somehow gained the advantage over her, maybe even killed her?

No. *No.*

The notion of a world without at least one of their parents still alive and involved in their lives was too horrible to contemplate. This is what he told himself. That he would refuse to even consider the idea. But the thoughts intruded again anyway, bringing him close to whimpering like a helpless child.

Then Chelsea spoke.

He glanced at her. "What?"

She'd turned her gaze his way for the first time since getting in the vehicle. Her eyes were focused and that blankness was gone from her expression. Except for the blood on her face, she looked almost normal, present and engaged again. "I said you're going too fast. You need to slow down. *Way* down."

Zach looked at the dash.

97 MPH.

The speed limit along this stretch of highway was 65. It would go up to 75 a few miles farther down the road. Either way, well in excess of what the law allowed. He failed to see how this was a problem. They were in a dire situation, one far bigger than such minor concerns.

"Mom said we could text her as soon as we get to Lakemoor. The faster we get there, the better."

Chelsea shook her head. "Zach, slow the hell down. I'm serious. You're going so fast you might get a reckless driving charge instead of just a speeding ticket if we get pulled over."

Zach huffed. "So fucking what? If we get pulled over, we can tell the cops what happened. They can help."

"No." Chelsea's tone was adamant. "Mom didn't say much, but we know she doesn't want us talking to the police. That was pretty clear. We have to respect her wishes. I mean it. I'll be so fucking pissed if you let it happen."

Zach struggled to make sense of Chelsea's stance on this matter. His paranoia was worsening by the moment and he was convinced they needed an immediate solution of any kind, some way this grave matter could be lifted from their shoulders and entrusted to more competent people. Adults. Serious people in positions of authority. Even as he had these thoughts, he knew it was a child-like instinct. He was afraid. Terribly afraid. The situation was too big for him and he didn't know how to handle it. Making it all worse was knowing his younger sister was now technically under his care, and he was deeply afraid he wouldn't be able to protect her should the need arise.

He took his foot off the accelerator and began to apply pressure to the brake, lightly at first and then in a firmer way. The Pathfinder's speed dropped well below 90 MPH as he maneuvered the vehicle out of the passing lane. He let out a breath as their speed continued to slide back toward a normal standard of acceptable highway travel, his state of agitation declining along with it.

Chelsea sighed. "Thank you."

Zach looked at her. "Are you okay? I was beginning to think you'd gone catatonic."

She shook her head. "I'm a long way from okay."

He nodded. "Yeah. That guy was fucking scary."

She grunted. "You don't know the half of it."

Something in her tone set Zach on edge. His head swiveled slowly toward her. "What do you mean?"

She sniffled. "He handled me roughly before you came in the house, knocking me around and . . . stuff."

A new sense of horror rose inside Zach, along with a wish to return to their house and kill the man himself. "You don't mean . . ."

He couldn't say it.

She wiped a tear away. "He didn't rape me, but I think maybe only because he didn't have time. You got there only about ten minutes after he did. He smacked me around and asked about Dad. Of course I couldn't tell him anything. Then he held me against him, groping me and whispering revolting things in my ear. When he heard you coming in, he shoved me down in that chair and put the gun to my head."

"That fucking bastard."

Chelsea sniffled again. "Yeah."

They lapsed back into silence after that, Chelsea weeping quietly while Zach stewed in his burgeoning anger. Some twenty-odd minutes later, the green exit sign for Lakemoor came into view. Just beyond it was another sign, a blue one with symbols indicating the presence of gas stations and fast food restaurants just off the highway.

Zach's foot returned to the brake as he put on the SUV's blinker. In a few more moments, they were off the highway and gliding along the curving white exit ramp. Less than a minute later, he steered them into the parking lot of a mid-sized convenience store. There were some empty parking spaces right out front, but Zach drove around to the smaller strip of spaces at the side of the store. He was hoping for some privacy while attempting to reestablish contact with their mother.

He grabbed his phone from the tray under the radio and sent a quick, simple text: *We're in Lakemoor.*

He stared hard at the screen, willing its status to quickly change from "delivered" to "read", but this did not immediately occur. The screen dimmed and he tapped it to keep it from going dark. This happened a few more times without the status of the message changing. After the fifth time, his anxiety began to ramp upward again. The time after that he muttered a curse and started squirming in his seat. He tried to calm down by rationalizing that only a handful of minutes had passed. Of course he'd hoped for an immediate reply, but the lack of one didn't necessarily mean anything bad. Their mother could be straightening things out with the police and thus unable to answer or even look at her phone. It might be a while yet.

The screen dimmed again. He tapped it again.

Delivered.

Never in his life had so ordinary a word seemed so hateful.

"Jesus, Zach, you need to calm the hell down. You look like a death row inmate about to be walked into the execution chamber."

Zach frowned as he glanced at her. "Gee, I'm so sorry. I'm fucking worried as hell about Mom. You almost seem like you're taking this in stride, like it's no big deal. I don't get how that's possible. Why aren't you freaking out like me?"

Chelsea looked hurt. "God, I'm not taking anything in stride. I'm worried too. But we need to keep our heads on straight for Mom's sake. She's probably just as worried about us as we are about her."

Zach wasn't so sure about that.

He thought about the way Noreen Murphy had hurried them out

of the house and sent them away. Something about her demeanor during those moments nagged at him, something beyond the obvious, but at first he'd been unable to nail down exactly what it was. As he sat there and stared at the phone while the minutes continued to pass, something began to click in his head, his first faint inkling of what was bothering him.

He looked up and craned his head around, not looking for anything in particular but instead attempting to focus his thinking by not staring at the phone. Some people were standing at the gas pumps while filling up their cars. A minivan pulled into the parking lot and drove toward the front of the store, circumventing the pumps. No one was looking their way. The Pathfinder was just another anonymous vehicle among several here, the distress of its occupants hidden from the outside world. It felt kind of weird, this ongoing sense of his entire world unraveling, a massively momentous thing perceived by no one in the vicinity.

Then it came to him.

He saw their mother's face in his head again, an image in ultrahigh definition. His concentration intensified as he continued to recall how she'd looked during those moments of extreme tension. He'd seen worry etched in those features, yes, but also a high degree of impatience. She wanted her kids to get to a safe place, but she also wanted them out of the way so she could . . . do something. This in itself wasn't a total revelation. He'd considered a lot of possibilities regarding her intentions and one was that she hadn't wanted them around to see her execute the man in cold blood by firing another bullet into his head.

One that wouldn't just graze him.

Zach looked at his phone.

Delivered.

No reply yet.

"*Fuck.*"

"It's only been a little over ten minutes."

Zach nodded, his gaze staying on the phone rather than going to Chelsea. "I know, but the wait is driving me crazy. I feel like I might lose my mind soon."

Chelsea groaned. "So stop looking at your phone. Let it go for a few minutes. Go in the store and get a Coke or something. I could use some wet wipes to clean the blood off my face. It feels sticky and nasty and I want it off my skin. Could you please do that for me? I can't go in looking like this or I'd do it myself."

Zach let out a long sigh. "Okay. Yeah, I can do that. Will you be okay by yourself for a few minutes?"

A hint of a smile lifted the corners of her mouth a tiny fraction. "I don't think I'm about to have a breakdown or anything if that's what you mean. Go on. I'll be fine."

"Okay, as long as you're sure."

"I'm sure."

After telling her to keep the doors locked, he got out of the SUV and went into the store. As soon as he pushed the door open and stepped inside, he realized he'd left his phone in the vehicle. He considered running back to the SUV to retrieve it but decided against it. He'd only be in this place a few minutes.

The middle-aged clerk behind the counter gave him a nasty look. He had long salt-and-pepper hair and a large beer gut that strained the front of his store smock. A lady in a flowery sundress stepped up to the counter with a handful of items and set them down, diverting the clerk's attention.

Zach moved away from the front of the store and roved up and down the narrow aisles until he found the wet wipes. Making a mental note of their location, he ducked into the bathroom in the back. He'd abruptly realized how badly he needed to piss. Once that was taken care of, he washed his hands and hurried out of the bathroom. He grabbed two packs of wet wipes and two bottles of Coke and headed up to the counter. Two other customers were in front of him, waiting to check out. One was a rather large woman holding a child who couldn't be more than a year old. Another child, a toddler wearing the world's littlest Kid Rock T-shirt, stood at her side sucking his thumb.

The woman was second in line.

Her free hand was empty.

Zach considered this ominous, a suspicion confirmed when she stepped up to the counter and started telling the clerk about all the Powerball tickets she wanted to buy. She took out a scrap of paper with some numbers scrawled on it and started slowly reading them off to him.

This was taking longer than he'd hoped. He started getting antsy as the woman continued reading off the numbers. The toddler in the Kid Rock shirt scowled at him and flipped him off. A part of him ached to return the gesture in kind, but he didn't want any part of the trouble that might cause. Too much time was passing. His anxiety level was so high he felt like he might jump out of his skin at any moment.

Then, at long last, the woman dug a wallet out of the large, over-flowing purse hanging by a strap from her shoulder.

Zach heaved a sigh of immense relief.

Fucking finally.

He was just stepping up to the counter when he heard the gunshot ring out from the parking lot.

SEVEN

A FEELING OF OVER-SATIATION rendered Noreen woozy after she at last disengaged herself from the corpse of the hunter. She wandered about the kitchen in a daze for several moments, dripping blood all over the floor. Her thoughts were too disordered, like her head was a box filled with puzzle parts that wouldn't quite fit together. She looked from the refrigerator to the microwave oven on the counter to the table and then at the savaged corpse on the floor, unsure of what to do next. An awareness of a need for urgency lurked in the background, awaiting her return to clarity.

This was how it'd always been in the old days, back when draining a human being to the point of expiration was a regular thing. Her brain was so overstimulated it was misfiring, rendered briefly incapable of forming the countless intricate connections that made cogent thought possible. The key word there was "briefly" because, also like in the old days, the feeling of incapacitating overstimulation didn't last long.

Less than two minutes after getting to her feet, everything snapped back into sharp focus. Her nervous system felt electrified but no longer overstimulated. She was an intelligent woman by any ordinary standard, but the large influx of blood elevated her perceptions and brought a clarity of thought far beyond her normal abilities.

She felt as if her IQ had been boosted by fifty points or more. The effect of the blood infusion was in no way limited to mental acuity. She felt vastly stronger than before. Powerful like a goddess, able to physically rip a man's body in half should the need arise.

Her heightened senses allowed her to perceive the dangerous presence nearby. She rushed into the foyer and peered around the edge of a curtain as two police cruisers rolled up and parked in front of the house. They'd arrived without their flashers going, pulling up smoothly with minimal noise rather than screeching to a halt after tearing down the street. Noreen assumed this was done in the interest of not panicking any armed person who might be in the house.

She had no direct knowledge of standard police procedure in these situations, yet she intuited what was in the heads of the officers so easily it was nearly akin to reading their minds. Their agitation was palpable. She could almost feel the sweat oozing from their pores, sensed how on edge they were as they remained in their cruisers for several minutes. Despite the caution they'd exhibited thus far, they had to know a confrontation of some kind would occur soon. Multiple 911 reports of shots fired in this nice neighborhood wasn't something that could be ignored or waited out until the danger had passed. She felt them psyching themselves up, getting ready.

A cruiser door opened and one of the officers emerged from the vehicle, squinting against the bright sunlight. Then others got out and they all spent a few additional moments huddling together, occasionally glancing at the house in a grim, worried way.

Dealing with them in any fashion wasn't a viable option.

There was a large dead man on the floor of her kitchen. A man who'd been shot twice before having his throat ripped open. A large pool of blood had spread out around his unmoving form. Noreen's face and chest were covered in crimson. There was a bullet hole in one of the French door windows. The men from the cruisers were walking toward the house. She had no hope of concealing this ample evidence of carnage or cleaning herself off before they arrived.

Only one solution existed.

After wiping off her feet and soaking up some of the worst of the drippy places from her skin with a dish towel, she walked out of the kitchen. She left her heels on the bloody floor and ignored the clothes she'd left draped over a chair as she descended a short set of steps to the adjacent den. Those items would not serve her well for what was to come and she'd ruin the dress if she donned it now anyway. The only thing she took with her was her purse. Even the Ruger was left behind.

The den was where the Murphy family had always spent the bulk of its leisure time. As she entered the cozy space, images of her kids lounging on the large sectional while playing games or watching movies on the big wall-mounted television flitted through her head. Memories of family movie nights in the days before Jonathan pulled his vanishing act, large bowls of extra buttery popcorn on the coffee table. The kids hanging out with their friends, the ones who didn't come over much anymore because the fun vibe that had once prevailed in this home had vanished along with Jonathan.

All of it was the past now, never to be restored.

Once she was gone from here today, she would never return. Nor would her kids. Nor would Jonathan. It was too late now for a miracle return from wherever he'd gone. That era of their lives was finished. The realization made her feel a deep bitterness, as well as a rage that was just beginning to build. Soon it would become all-consuming. That happy life had been stolen from all of them and there was more than one person responsible.

They would pay. Every single one of them.

The hunters.

The one who'd betrayed them.

Anyone else who got in her way. She was fully prepared to kill and kill again and keep on killing until she'd eliminated everyone who might feasibly stand in the way of getting her family out of this mess.

Noreen moved past the sectional and entered a short hallway. A door to the left opened into a rarely used guest bedroom with two twin beds. Before entering, she glanced behind her to examine the floor. Her efforts with the dish towel had been quick but efficient. There was no discernible blood trail. She entered the bedroom and closed the door.

In a corner at the rear of the room was a walk-in closet mainly used for storage. Old clothes no one had worn for years dangled from hangers on the racks. There were boxes of things on the floor and the shelves. Someone knocked stridently on the front door as she closed the door to the closet. She snatched a little black dress she hadn't worn in a decade from one of the hangers and grabbed a pair of frayed-looking red tennis shoes from the floor. Taking these items was incidental to her true purpose in coming to this particular closet.

This was her way out.

The rear wall of the closet retracted silently when she touched it in the right spot, sliding smoothly into a hidden recess that would be undetectable when the panel closed again. She stepped through the opening into a darkened space, where she touched a button on a keypad. The panel slid along its track until it was shut, leaving the usual appearance of seamlessness on the other side. She worked by feel and memory as she touched another button to deactivate automatic opening. Another button tap filled the small space with light.

This space was half the size of the closet. There were no windows here, no way for anyone to guess the soundproofed secret chamber existed. The light would not be visible to any of the cops who would soon be tearing through the house. Sealing herself in and merely waiting them out was one of her options. She could stay here until nighttime and slip away undetected after their investigation of the scene was complete. It would then be an easy thing to put in motion the emergency bug-out plan she and Jonathan had devised so long ago. They had a storage unit on the other side of town. The kids didn't know about it because they didn't know their parents were daywalkers, didn't even know such creatures existed, making them like the vast majority of the world's population in that regard.

The storage unit contained everything they would need to get a solid jump-start on beginning new lives elsewhere. Multiple sets of the highest quality fake identification cards and documents. A kitchen-sized refrigerator filled with blood-filled plastic pouches, enough to tide them over until they could start anew somewhere else and make arrangements with a new supplier. Also in the storage shed were packed suitcases, an impressive array of weaponry, burner phones, and something uniquely dangerous sealed inside an appropriate container. A thing that would have to be destroyed before she could safely move on.

There was also a car. An unassuming foreign compact registered to a person who at the moment existed only as a set of phony documents. It was an older car, but Jonathan had maintained it well until his disappearance. Once he was gone, Noreen had assumed maintenance duties, tending to the vehicle diligently ever since. Her last visit to the unit to ensure everything was in order had been just two days ago. All of this was done out of an abundance of caution, expecting the best but remaining prepared for the worst. Somehow she'd never truly believed the day would come when she would finally have to avail herself of those preparations.

Yet here she was. Hiding from the police. Knowing her life as she'd known it was at an end. It made her angry and sad at the same time. This was happening because Jonathan had taken off without warning or explanation. His vanishing had come as a complete surprise. She knew he was alive. He'd communicated with her for a few minutes at a time on a handful of occasions. Yet he still hadn't supplied her with an explanation. It was endlessly infuriating. She missed him with a desperation that was nearly suffocating at times, and at the same time she kind of hated him. Worst of all, he'd divulged knowledge every vampire knew no regular human should ever be entrusted with because of the high risk of betrayal.

Jonathan was a smart man. He knew these things, was fully cognizant of the risks, yet he did what he did anyway. Perhaps most unforgivable of all, he hadn't just done it to her, he'd done it to his kids, shattering their peaceful family life with his stupid indiscretion. There was a part of her that yearned to have an axe in her hands and his head on a chopping block.

Noreen dropped her purse on the floor and sat in the only chair in the room. In a corner was a small refrigerator of the type typically found in the dorm rooms of college students. Like the larger one in the storage unit, it was filled with blood pouches, relatively fresh. Locked inside a cabinet mounted on the wall opposite the hideaway's hidden entrance was an assortment of guns and ammunition. One was a Glock 19. She'd take that one with her whenever she was finally able to leave.

She unlocked her phone via facial recognition and accessed the home's video security system. There were hidden cameras in every room. The network's hub was in a closet inside her bastard husband's former office. There were monitors with a view of every room. Noreen was able to see everything the cameras showed on her phone. There was even crystal-clear sound.

The cops were freaking out. They were cursing a lot and making noises of disbelief and disgust. The disgust was mostly about the savaged condition of the dead man's throat. There was a lot of confusion about how it had happened. More than one of them thought it looked like the work of a wild animal, but that made no sense because the house was closed up tight and there was no such creature to be found. They were also pretty upset that all the home's actual residents were missing. It was inexplicable. The word "clusterfuck" was used numerous times.

She lost track of time as she watched them. There was one guy who seemed to be in charge. He stayed in the kitchen for the duration, sometimes speaking into the radio mic pinned to his uniform shirt. Other cops moved in and out of the kitchen around him. Some other personnel who weren't police officers eventually showed up. Technicians or medical examiners, she wasn't sure.

At last she got tired of watching the video feed and clicked out of it. It wouldn't be long before they discovered the network hub in the closet and shut it off anyway. Only then did she think to check her messages. She saw a few from various friends and acquaintances. They'd all heard about the incident at her house and were trying to reach her. Why any of them thought she'd respond under the circumstances she did not know.

There was only one message that mattered.

We're in Lakemoor.

Zach had sent it from his phone sixteen minutes earlier.

Noreen grimaced.

She wished she'd had the time and foresight to better advise her son about what to say and what not to say upon arriving at his destination. Specifying his location in a text was an unfortunate thing, but she couldn't blame him for not taking this most basic of precautions. He didn't think like a criminal, and she couldn't expect him to anticipate other steps he should take to avoid apprehension.

Noreen did not send an immediate reply.

She felt bad about it because the time stamp on Zach's message meant he'd already been waiting a while to hear back from her. The delay in responding would worry him. She wanted nothing more than to offer immediate reassurance, but she needed another minute to think things through first.

Somehow she needed to communicate to her kids how much more dire the situation had become and convey instructions about how to proceed, but she couldn't do the latter without the cops becoming aware of her plans.

At some point, before too much longer, a coordinated police effort to locate her children would begin. Their phones would be pinged. Other data, including texts, might be retrieved, though that part could take a little longer. Likely not a whole lot longer, though. The only thing she could think to do was call the kids and tell them they would have to destroy or dump their phones. They would then have to get back out on the interstate and drive another town or two farther away, and she would have to catch up to them later tonight.

Then she thought of another problem. The Pathfinder's built-in GPS, also potentially accessible to the police after going through the necessary procedures.

Fuck!

Noreen's frustration level skyrocketed again.

She was still fretting over it when another text came in from Zach: *mom where are u Chelsea shot some guy!!!*

EIGHT

ZACH BANGED THROUGH THE CONVENIENCE store's front doors and stumbled out onto the sidewalk, wheeling about off-balance while flailing his arms in an effort to remain upright. Both of his feet were right at the edge of the sidewalk, and he could feel himself beginning to pitch forward, his likely landing spot the hood of the lime-green Mazda right in front of him.

Someone behind him was yelling. Whoever it was sounded really pissed off. Only then did he realize he still had the items he hadn't paid for gripped in his hands. That explained the yelling. The store clerk thought he was robbing the place. Why Zach hadn't simply dropped everything upon hearing the gunshot, he did not know.

His desperate flailing miraculously kept him from landing on the Mazda's hood, the pinwheeling motion of his body carrying him away from the edge of the sidewalk before it was too late. After an additional awkward extra step or two, he got his feet set properly beneath him and ran fast toward the side of the building.

As soon as he rounded the corner, he came to a dead stop and gasped at what he saw. A burly redheaded man dressed all in black was dead on the pavement a few feet away from the Pathfinder. The closed driver-side window had been blown out by the bullet fired from the gun gripped in Chelsea's shaking hands. A glance at the dead man showed a bloody hole formerly occupied by his right eye. A shotgun was on the ground at his side. Not for the first time that afternoon, Zach experienced a surreal and dizzying sense of disorientation.

This made two one-eyed interlopers—intent on fucking up their lives—they'd had to deal with within a very short span of time. The odds against that ever happening to anyone who wasn't a spy or combat soldier had to be astronomical, perhaps almost beyond calculation. The lottery lady who'd aggravated him so much in the store had better odds of winning the Powerball. Of course this second dude had only become one-eyed posthumously, but it was still mind-boggling.

Someone came to a skidding stop behind Zach and shrieked in shock, presumably at the sight of the body. A glance over his shoulder revealed the shrieker as the store clerk.

The middle-aged man's eyes bulged.

He looked from the body to Zach's face and then to the SUV, where he saw Chelsea still holding the gun in both hands in an upraised firing position. From the clerk's vantage point, it would appear as if she were now aiming the gun at him. Or just in his general direction, which would be plenty scary enough for any normal person.

The clerk's face went pale.

Then his eyes rolled back and his body began to wobble. He staggered backward a few steps and then tried to move sideways. Another second later he collapsed to the ground. His head lolled to one side, mouth hanging open.

He'd fainted.

Zach considered this a not entirely unreasonable reaction to the situation. Unfortunately, unlike the clerk, he did not have the luxury of swooning like some fragile damsel in an old movie. Things had just gone from merely bad and scary to absolutely terrifying in the most gut-twisting, ball-shriveling way imaginable.

He looked out at the parking lot and saw a handful of people gawking at the scene, but they were keeping their distance, some staying partially hidden behind gas pumps. Whatever else happened next, Zach knew he couldn't keep standing here. Now that Chelsea had shot and killed a man in broad daylight in a public place, voluntarily giving themselves up to the police no longer felt like a good option.

"*Zach!*"

Chelsea, screaming at him, sounding impatient.

Zach stood rooted to the spot another second longer. Chelsea screamed again, the sound shrill and laced with a sharper note of desperation.

His first step toward the SUV was a halting one. Then he got moving faster. He saw Chelsea lean across the seat and throw the door open for him, allowing him to vault up into the vehicle. His head bumped against the edge of the roof, but it was a glancing blow that barely slowed him down. The items from the store were still in his hands. He dumped them in Chelsea's lap and got himself properly settled behind the steering wheel.

After pulling the door shut, he dug the keys out of his pocket and jabbed the key for the Pathfinder at the ignition slot, missing it twice before it slid home. The extra couple seconds this required made him wish the SUV was one of the newer models with keyless ignition, but this one was fully paid off and in excellent running condition. Noreen Murphy would have considered changing it out for a new one a waste of money. Zach believed she might have had a different opinion if she could have foreseen this moment.

He got the Pathfinder started and backed out of the parking space, changed gears, cranked the steering wheel around, and hit the gas. The SUV shot forward and raced toward the street, barely slowing down as they turned out of the parking lot.

Zach hadn't gone far before realizing his mistake. He was heading into Lakemoor instead of back toward the interstate. His foot went to the brake pedal as he allowed the SUV to drift to the shoulder. The plan here was to make a wide, looping turn in the middle of the two-lane road instead of wasting time looking for a proper turnaround point. He was just beginning to twist the steering wheel when Chelsea lunged at him and grabbed hold of it.

"Stop!"

Zach's foot jammed down on the brake, bringing the vehicle to a full stop. He could feel his heart racing way faster than normal as his anxiety kicked back into high gear. Was that a faint sound of sirens emanating from some distant point he was just beginning to hear?

Maybe. Some kind of barely perceptible whine, for sure.

It got a little louder.

He glared at his sister. "What are you doing? We've gotta get the fuck out of this town."

Chelsea shook her head. "No, Zach, *think*. If we'd gone out to the highway, those people would have told the cops and they'd have us stopped in no time. We have to keep going this way, I'm fucking serious."

Zach groaned.

There was no time to debate the wisdom of one course versus another. Besides, his sister was right and he should have seen it from the start. The interstate was a trap. They'd be easier to spot from the air. There'd be far fewer ways of possibly slipping away. The appeal of the interstate was speed, but that wouldn't matter if they were unable to duck out of sight when necessary or shake pursuers.

He took his foot off the brake, pulled back onto the road, and hit the gas again.

"Okay, so what now? Things have changed. You know that, right? It's not just what Mom did or didn't do at the house we have to worry about. You shot some dude. *Killed* him. We're gonna have about a million cops on our ass soon."

Chelsea sighed heavily and stared out at the road ahead. Her face looked blank. Zach flashed back to how she'd seemed almost catatonic earlier, back out there on the interstate. She hadn't been like that for long, but he couldn't help worrying she might lapse back into that mode.

He tore his gaze away from her and glanced out at the stretch of rural road ahead of them. Tall trees with heavy green canopies leaned toward the road from both sides. There were no houses or other buildings. Coming up on the right he spied a rusted mailbox on a crooked wooden post. Next to it was a narrow dirt drive, but if anyone was still living back there, they were well out of sight.

Chelsea sat up, instantly more alert upon spotting the mailbox. "We should turn in there."

Zach looked at the rearview mirror.

He slowed the SUV as he considered the suggestion. They hadn't put nearly enough distance between themselves and the convenience store to feel safe about stopping anywhere yet. No more than slightly over a mile had rolled off on the odometer. Basic common sense told him stopping here, at the first available turnoff, would be a colossally stupid thing to do. It'd be little different from giving themselves up to the cops.

Wouldn't it?

He applied a bit more pressure to the brake, bringing the SUV's speed down to 20 MPH. That rising whine in the distance was sirens, he was sure of it now. Still some distance away but getting closer. The time remaining to think and make a decision was down to almost nothing.

Zach looked again at the rearview mirror.

They hadn't traveled far, it was true, but now he'd noticed the road leading away from the store wasn't a straight line but a gently curving one. It had curved just enough, in fact, to hide the store and the interstate junction beyond it from view.

Before he could decide anything, Zach caught sight of a slate-gray sedan approaching from the direction of town. It was traveling at a sedate speed and was still too far away to make out much about it other than basic vehicle type. He couldn't know for sure until it was closer, but he didn't think the approaching car was a police cruiser. The slow speed was indicative of someone who was either elderly or not confident in their driving abilities.

Zach slowed the Pathfinder to a near full stop.

Chelsea glanced at him, frowning. "We can't turn in here now. Whoever's driving that car will remember and tell the police."

The slow-moving sedan was still gliding along the road's gentle curve, far enough away to allow Zach a little more time to think as a wild and impulsive plan began to take shape in his head. There was a strong element of recklessness to it and he feared its likelihood of success wasn't very high, but a big element of desperation was in play. Getting out of this mess would require taking chances, maybe a lot of them.

The Pathfinder was stopped now.

Zach wrenched the gear shifter over to P.

He looked at Chelsea. "Give me the gun."

Her frown became more pronounced. "What? Why?"

He held out his hand. "Just give it to me."

She met his gaze and something in her responded to his tone and expression.

She put the gun in his hand.

He let out a breath. "Get out and come around to my side."

He opened the door and stepped out into the street. Chelsea came around the front of the SUV and was at his side within a couple seconds. The approaching car was no more than twenty yards away. The sound of sirens was much louder now and still seemed to only be emanating from the direction of the store. It was doubtful that would remain the case for much longer.

Chelsea met his gaze again. "What are we doing?"

Zach put the gun against the small of her back and gave her a little push. "Step into the lane and wave your hands like we're having an emergency."

He expected her to ask him why, but she didn't hesitate.

Chelsea stepped into the other lane and waved her arms in a frantic motion above her head, moving several feet up the street toward the approaching vehicle, which slowed to a crawl. Zach moved with his sister, staying right behind her as he kept the gun out of sight.

The car didn't come to a full stop until its front bumper was no more than two feet from Chelsea, who was crying and loudly pleading for help. Some degree of acting might have been involved in this display, but Zach figured probably not much. She'd been through a lot in a short time and was likely feeling crushed by the weight of it all. Zach himself felt right on the trembling edge of a total emotional breakdown but, for the time being at least, the feeling was overridden by the urgency of the moment.

An elderly woman sat behind the wheel of the old Ford Taurus. She hit a button to lower her window. A warbly voice screeched at them to get the hell out of the road. Her tone spurred something in Zach, erasing any remaing hesitation to do this crazy thing.

He moved fast and stuck the gun through the open window, pressing the muzzle against her wrinkled forehead. "I'm sorry to have to do this, granny, but I'm commandeering this car."

She screeched again and swatted at him as he leaned over her and grabbed hold of the shifter with his free hand. Once the car was in park, he opened the door, unbuckled the woman's seatbelt, and roughly shoved her over to the passenger seat. This gave rise to more screeching and swatting, but Zach was able to drop in behind the steering wheel.

He stuck the gun in her face again. "Shut up or die."

She looked eager to unleash another screeching tirade, but the feel of the cold muzzle pressed against her eye appeared to make her reconsider. Chelsea approached the Taurus and leaned down to peer in at her brother.

"What are we doing?"

Zach stuck the gun between his legs. "The keys are still in the Pathfinder. Get in and follow me into the woods. Be fucking quick about it. We're almost out of time."

He shifted gears and turned the Taurus in the direction of the rust-flecked old mailbox. Sirens were coming from both directions now.

They were almost out of time. He tapped the gas and headed for the narrow dirt road next to the mailbox.

Seconds later, Chelsea followed.

The Taurus jostled Zach and the elderly woman as its wheels bounced over uneven ruts and dipped in and out of various depressions in the path, which was so narrow that low-hanging tree branches scratched against both sides of the vehicle. The scratching resulted in an unnerving screeching sound, like a violin played by a deranged musical novice.

The old woman fumed. "You're ruining my paint job."

"Sorry."

"You'll go to jail for this."

Zach sighed.

That's a distinct possibility.

After what felt like forever, the dirt path came to an end and the Taurus emerged into a small clearing. A dilapidated old shack sat at the back of the clearing. The squat little building looked to have been constructed utilizing a wide range of odds and ends. Mismatched pieces of lumber, plywood, logs, and even some fiberglass panels. The pieces had been crudely mortared together. There were two windows in the front, but the glass was broken out. A rusted shell of an ancient Studebaker pickup truck rested next to the shack. The truck's wheels were missing. The tattered remnants of an old Confederate battle flag hung from the porch rail, the bottom stirred by the slight breeze.

Zach grimaced.

The place looked sketchy as hell. No one was around, at least no one he could see, and a part of him hoped like hell they hadn't arrived just in time for a chainsaw massacre.

Because this definitely looked like the sort of place where a chainsaw massacre might occur.

Zach pulled up to the cabin and turned the Taurus around, getting the front end pointed back in the direction of the narrow path. Chelsea drove the Pathfinder into the clearing and parked next to the rusted-out Studebaker without bothering to turn it around. That was good. She was intuitively understanding what he had in mind, which would hopefully help them move faster and better their chances of getting away.

Chelsea emerged from the SUV within seconds of coming to a stop. His backpack was slung over her shoulder. She also had the still unopened bottles of Coke and the wet wipes.

In her other hand was his phone.

He could hear it ringing from across the clearing.

Chelsea hurried over to the open driver-side window of the Taurus and thrust the phone at Zach. The word *Mom* appeared on the screen.

He answered the call and put the phone to his ear.

After listening to his mother talk fast for about thirty seconds, he said, "Already ahead of you on that count, believe it or not."

He sketched out what had happened and what they'd done as quickly as he could.

A beat of silence from the other end. Zach couldn't help smiling as he imagined her surprise, knowing she would not have expected him capable of such a daring move. There was also likely some shock regarding the gas station incident, but the silence was short-lived as she launched back into fast-talking mode, telling him what else they needed to do. Some of it was stuff he'd already guessed, but there were also things he hadn't thought of yet, things that should have been obvious.

She told him to move fast.

Then she told him she had to go.

The line went dead.

Zach stuck the gun in the trembling old woman's face again. "You're gonna need to get out of the car now, granny."

He hated to sound so harsh and threatening.

This was an innocent person. Not only that, but a frail elderly lady. He worried he might literally frighten her to death. She'd wound up in this unfortunate position by random chance. She didn't deserve this. No one did.

But it was happening anyway.

Feeling bad about it didn't change what Zach knew he had to do. Saving his sister and himself was what mattered most. He could wallow in his guilt later, *if* there was a later.

There were a bunch of old bungee cords in the back of the Pathfinder. They used them to bind the woman and stash her in the rear of the vehicle.

Chelsea finally ripped open a pack of wet wipes and used them to clear away as much of the blood from her face as she could manage in just a couple minutes.

Then they got in the Taurus and drove back out to the street.

This time Chelsea was behind the wheel.

NINE

NOREEN STARED BLANKLY AT HER phone for at least a minute after ending the call with her son. She would move mountains to reunite with her kids, transgress against any and all of society's rules if that's what it took. All that mattered was being with them again, making things right again somehow.

Despite all that, a nagging voice of worry and doubt whispered dark and distressing things to her from a region of her mind less colored by emotion. A part that couldn't help wondering if she'd just heard her son's voice for the last time. The thought elicited a shiver of dread. It also sparked a fresh surge of quivering rage, causing her to grip the phone so tightly it felt close to snapping in half.

This was no false impression. The amplified strength she'd derived from draining the dead hunter's blood hadn't ebbed. She'd be buzzing with it for many hours to come after so massive an overindulgence. She could crush the phone in her hand as easily as she'd wad up a scrap of paper. In fact, she'd have to do it before leaving this place. She couldn't take it with her because it would serve as a beacon, leading the police to anywhere she went. Leaving it intact in this secret space also wasn't a good option. She didn't want the hidden room discovered in the unlikely event she ever needed an undetectable way back into the house.

She increased the pressure of her hand against the sides of the phone and felt the fragile casing beginning to give way. One more slight increase of pressure and it would yield to the force she was exerting.

Then she made herself relax her grip.

On impulse she swiped back over to the app connecting the phone to the security monitoring system. There were still cops and technicians standing around in the kitchen. The cops didn't appear to be doing much, just hanging out while techs went about their business. Now and then the main cop guy would respond to someone on his radio mic.

She started clicking through views of other rooms in the house, stopping when she landed on one showing the guest bedroom. Two uniformed officers were in the room. Both were musclebound goons who looked like they spent far more time pumping iron in the gym than busting criminals, but their physical mass didn't intimidate Noreen. Even in the absence of her blood-enhanced super strength, she would feel confident in her ability to handle any foe. It might be more physically difficult and result in a lot of messy chaos, but she could do it.

She stared at the screen as the brawny cops tore the room apart, upending both twin beds and yanking all the drawers out of the dresser. One of them went to the closet and looked inside. Despite not fearing these men as physical opponents, it was disquieting to know they were only a few feet away. The one peering into the closet moved all the way into it as she watched. He slid the old clothes along the rack and inspected the space beneath, looking for who-knew-what. At the back of the closet, he turned around and stood with his broad back to the rear wall. He was approximately three feet from where Noreen sat in the metal folding chair.

She sighed.

Enough.

It was time to go.

She'd done all she could from within the confines of her hiding place.

Her purse was a large one, which was fortunate because it would serve her purposes from this point forward. It was more accurate to call it a handbag or tote. When she was younger, she'd favored smaller, almost dainty-looking bags because they were cute and fashionable. As a mother, bags of that sort became impractical. There'd been times when she'd lamented surrendering certain aspects of her former self to the realities of motherhood, but today was not one of those days.

She snatched the bag off the floor and shoved in the little black dress and red sneakers she'd grabbed from the closet. Rising from the chair, she went to the gun cabinet and opened it, taking out the Glock 19, two boxes of ammunition, and a spare magazine. These also went in the bag. She took multiple blood pouches from the mini-fridge and piled them atop everything else. Next she dragged the fridge away from the corner, the power cord coming loose from the wall outlet as she slid the appliance into the middle of the room. This revealed the outline of a trapdoor.

She hadn't gone down to the tunnel below in years, not since Jonathan finished excavating and installing the support beams that kept the narrow passage from collapsing. He'd wanted her to traverse the length of it back and forth at least one time so she'd know what she was getting into should she ever need to make use of it.

That long ago test run had not been pleasant. It was not possible to walk either standing erect or hunched over in the tunnel. Crawling was the only option. This meant there was no way to avoid encountering a variety of insects along with the occasional rodent. She was no meek little housewife who squealed at the sight of a mouse. Obviously. She still had the blood of a man whose throat she'd ripped out all over her body. That didn't mean she was in any hurry to have rats or cockroaches or whatever crawling all over her, but the sooner she got on with it, the sooner she'd be done. And she'd be one step closer to being with her kids again.

Nonetheless she hesitated another moment longer, grabbing yet another blood bag from the mini-fridge. While the current blood buzz wouldn't be fading any time soon, she saw no reason not to top herself off with another dose before embarking on her mission. The packaged stuff wouldn't be quite as high octane as the fresh blood straight from the source she'd already consumed, but it would do the job well enough.

She ripped open a corner of the pouch with her teeth and began to slurp down the delicious red elixir. The bag was thick and filled to a point just shy of bursting, as they always were. Some of it spilled down her chin and dripped onto her chest. Feeling blood slide down her bare flesh had a familiar effect, a strong wave of arousal, one that frustratingly could not be satiated at the moment. Awareness of this added fuel to her always simmering resentment and hatred of Jonathan for what he'd done. She wanted him inside of her, almost more than she wanted to be with her kids again.

It was a dilemma.

She wanted to kill him.

She wanted to fuck him.

If she ever saw him again, she didn't know which she'd rather do. Maybe both.

Thinking this way was nearly as invigorating as the fresh infusion of blood. It was like tapping into a version of herself that had gone dormant long ago, one suddenly resurfacing after she'd believed it buried forever. At first it felt strange to feel the things she was feeling again, that old razor-edge wildness that had filled so many of her days and nights in the early years after Jonathan took away her humanity, turning her into a daywalker. That thrilling time before children and responsibility, when she'd hunted fresh prey and fed as she pleased, giving herself over to reckless abandon again and again.

Suppressing that version of herself had felt like the right thing to do. Jonathan's cautionary tales of the hunters who worked to exterminate their kind had tempered her ravening bloodlust. She came to believe he was right about creating a life for themselves that would not draw attention. A well-ordered, ordinary life. A veil of normality. It was their way of shielding themselves from the potential consequences of the things they'd done, and they'd done many, many bad things, not all of them against ordinary humans. They had far more dangerous enemies. Creatures they'd wronged, who'd love to capture and kill them. They had many reasons to hide and so they had, and it had worked for a long time. No one ever tracked them down. Until today. The anger she felt at having the veneer torn away was still present, but there was another part of her that welcomed its destruction.

Noreen dropped the empty blood bag on the floor. As her gaze returned to the trapdoor, she thought about the one the one-eyed man had called the Annihilator. The supposed super hunter his bosses sent in to clean up the messier cases. She'd been skeptical at first, but by the end she knew better. She knew what a dying man sounded like when he wasn't telling the truth.

The Annihilator was real and he was coming for them all. Noreen didn't exactly fear the phantom figure. She saw no reason she couldn't defeat him as easily as she'd defeat any mortal man. But the way the dead hunter had talked about him had instilled a slight sense of unease. It would be for the best if she could catch up to her kids and usher them out of the area before the Big, Scary Man arrived.

After again retrieving her handbag from the floor, Noreen opened the trapdoor and began her descent.

TEN

ANOTHER POLICE CRUISER WITH ITS roof lights strobing flashed by out on the street as Chelsea guided the Ford Taurus back down the narrow path leading away from the run-down shack. She squirmed in her seat, whimpering and saying "Oh my God" over and over. Her hands trembled as she gripped the steering wheel, feeling anxious as she was overcome with doubt about her ability to remain calm and make the right moves if things got crazy.

She drove the Taurus up to the edge of the road, shivering in relief upon seeing no vehicles approaching from either direction. Spinning the wheel to the right, she drove the vehicle out onto the street, giving it some gas as she headed toward Lakemoor and away from the interstate.

Her brother was in the trunk of the Taurus, per their mother's instructions. The reasoning was at least twofold—although they were now in a new vehicle not connected to them, a first step of supreme importance, they were still a young brother and sister traveling together, which was what the police would be on the lookout for. Even in a commandeered vehicle, they might draw attention. A young girl driving alone, however, had a better chance of going unnoticed by cops. Zach hadn't been all that thrilled about the idea, but he'd offered little in the way of protest, recognizing it as the smart thing to do under the circumstances.

Chelsea understood the logic behind the scheme and believed what their mother had in mind could work if nothing else went wrong, but understanding it did little to allay her fears. She was three weeks from turning seventeen, still just a kid in the eyes of many. Her driver's license had only been obtained a few months ago. She didn't have a car of her own and therefore still had little real-world practical driving experience. Not every cop in Lakemoor would be at the scene of the store shooting. At least a few traffic cops would still be on regular patrol. She feared making some dumb mistake that would cause one of them to attempt a traffic stop. Just the thought of it brought her close to hyperventilating because she honestly didn't know what she'd do if that happened.

She'd shot and killed a man.

She still couldn't believe it.

Sure, it'd been in self-defense. Yes, she'd perceived the man as an armed bad guy, one who meant to cause her harm, a view for which there was ample evidence. Regardless, she was pretty sure law enforcement frowned on shooting a man dead and fleeing the scene no matter the circumstances. They would expect her to stick around and explain herself at the very least.

The man had come from seemingly out of nowhere while she looked at her phone and waited for Zach to come out of the store, rapping on the driver-side window so hard it startled her into dropping her phone. She remembered looking at the guy and knowing instantly he was another one like the one-eyed man, a colleague who worked for the same people. Instinct told her he'd followed them out of the neighborhood. Maybe he'd been the one-eyed man's partner or something, waiting for him in the getaway car while One-Eye took care of the dirty work. It sounded plausible, but she'd never know for sure because, again, she'd already killed the son of a bitch.

Dead men tell no tales.

He'd started yelling at her through the closed window, his voice so loud he sounded like he was in the car with her instead of standing outside of it. She sat frozen in fear in the passenger seat of the SUV for several moments as he continued to yell at her, only snapping out of it when he tapped the barrel of his shotgun against the window and made a lewd comment that reminded her of the way One-Eye had treated her.

What happened next was sheer impulse.

She lunged through the gap between the seats, opened her brother's backpack, and found the gun her mother had stashed inside it. She flipped the safety off as she fell back into her seat and aimed it at the hulking, black-clad man.

She remembered the way he'd squinted at her in puzzlement for a moment before smirking.

His laughter had an unmistakably dismissive tinge to it as he again tapped the barrel of the shotgun against the window and said, "Come on, sweet thing, you know you're not gonna shoot me."

Chelsea did it without thinking, her finger twitching on the trigger. *BAM!*

The noise the gun made was far bigger than she expected, and the recoil surprised her, nearly shaking the weapon free of her two-handed grip. What she felt in those next few moments was mostly disbelieving shock. It seemed impossible that she'd actually done what she'd done. But the smirking man in black was no longer standing outside the blown-out window.

He was no longer laughing.

No longer menacing her.

He'd never menace anyone again, in fact.

Then Zach was there, shock also evident in his wide-eyed expression. She would not have been surprised to see him keel over just like the store clerk, but that didn't happen and it seemed almost like a miracle. He snapped out of it fast and got them out of there. She loved her brother, but the truth was she'd always seen him as kind of a weak-willed guy, far more beta than alpha, but it turned out there'd been a hidden stronger streak inside him all along.

The tree-shrouded road leading away from the convenience store went on for a while and she became antsy with the need to be off it. They needed significant separation from the store. Multiple turns onto other roads putting many miles of convoluted geographical distance between them and the scene of the crime would be ideal.

She could only hope she'd end up taking them in the right direction without taking any wrong turns along the way. GPS help would be nice, but they'd ditched their phones in the clearing. Again, this was on the advice of their mother. It was so the cops wouldn't be able to trace them. Also, leaving the phones where they had would eventually allow the cops to find the trussed-up old lady stashed in the back of the SUV.

Chelsea didn't feel great about the necessity of what they'd done to the woman, but truthfully it was only a secondary concern. She cared about her own safety and the safety of her brother above all other things, even if someone else had to suffer for it.

It was weird to feel this way.

So merciless. So ruthless.

She'd always prided herself on being a kind and considerate person, the kind of sweet girl who always tried to make others happy. Until today, she'd done precious little in her life that could fairly be described as "bad" or even mildly malicious.

And yet . . . there was maybe one little thing.

One small inkling she might not actually be a candidate for sainthood.

One of her best friends at school was a girl named Monica Ratcliffe. Monica was the prototypical mean girl, always saying catty things and cutting people down. She could be quite cruel at times. Sometimes when she was in Monica's presence, Chelsea found herself forced to cover her mouth to hide a smile or stifle a giggle at the nasty things her mean friend said. So maybe, just maybe, she'd harbored a darker side all along, one brought to the surface by today's traumatic turn of events. She had a bad feeling she might have to call on it again if they were to survive this shitty day.

The seemingly endless road finally came to an end, intersecting with another two-lane road, one with a new layer of blacktop so fresh it still looked wet. The divider line down the middle was a shade of newly painted yellow so bright it shimmered in the late afternoon sun. She saw a steady stream of passing cars heading in opposite directions. A glance at the rearview mirror showed no cars approaching from the rear, which helped settle her nerves. Reminding herself of the importance of adhering to the rules of the road, she turned on the right blinker. Less than a minute later, the gap in traffic she'd been waiting for finally appeared.

She hit the gas and turned right, speeding up a bit while being careful to go no faster than a few miles above the posted limit of 35 MPH.

No GPS meant she was forced to rely on memory as she drove according to her mother's directions as relayed to her by her brother. This presented a challenge as nearly all her previous solo driving experience had been GPS-assisted. Even most of her brief excursions to locations within her small hometown were made with that feminine robot voice telling her where to go. Being without it was so different it was almost surreal. It was old school, the way they'd done it in the prehistoric days of the twentieth century.

The stretch of road she was on now was similar to the previous one in that it was kind of desolate, with a big, open field to her left and a dense stand of trees beyond. No buildings of any kind. That seemed likely to change soon, given the number of vehicles passing through the area. She caught a glimpse of a traffic light directly ahead, some fifty feet distant. A few seconds later, as some of the cars ahead of her passed through the intersection, she spied a short turning lane to her left and slowed down as she eased the Taurus into it. She remembered to put on her blinker again right before coming to a full stop. Cars continued to flow through the intersection in both directions. Another car pulled in behind her, some old junker of a muscle car with a bad, noisy muffler.

The light was just starting to turn again, changing from green to yellow, when the intersection traffic finally began to clear. Her preference would have been to turn with a safely solid green light, but she didn't want to sit here and wait through another entire cycle of light changes and traffic. She stepped on the gas pedal and spun the wheel to the left, turning down yet another two-lane road. This time there were buildings, including a gas station and car wash to her right. A bit farther down was a Krystal's fast food restaurant. She stared at the sign with a surprising sense of longing. The little square burgers didn't normally appeal to her, but she'd skipped lunch. It was strange to feel hungry in the midst of a crisis, but the sudden need for food was there anyway.

She drove on by the restaurant, ignoring the temptation to pull in and quickly get something from the drive-thru. The longer they lingered here in Lakemoor, the worse their chances became of getting away. It was exactly the kind of stupid mistake she needed to avoid.

Their next turn was coming up in another few miles. She watched the odometer, remembering her mother's estimation of the distance. It'd be the last turn she'd have to make while still within the Lakemoor city limits because they'd then be on an old highway that predated the interstate system. From there it'd be a straight shot back to their hometown.

Chelsea glanced at the rearview mirror.

The old junker was still behind her, riding up annoyingly close to her rear bumper. It swerved slightly side to side while staying within the lane. She couldn't decide whether this was a signal of impatience regarding her speed or a display of aggression. The noise from the broken muffler sounded like the throaty roar of some predatory creature. As she watched, the junker did that swerving thing again, and this time the vibe she was getting did feel overtly aggressive in nature.

She couldn't see the driver because the junker's windows were tinted, but she felt pretty sure the person behind the wheel was a guy. Yeah, there were exceptions to every rule, but most girls she knew wouldn't drive like that for fear of inciting the ire of a potentially violent male.

At first, she'd given the junker little thought beyond how obnoxiously noisy it was, but now her paranoia began to surge. Since turning onto this road, they'd passed multiple other places where the junker could have turned instead of staying on her ass like this. That in itself didn't mean much. The driver could simply be in a hurry to get to the old highway, which was surely a well-used road.

Or he was a predator who'd clocked a young teenage girl driving around alone—or apparently alone anyway—and was now targeting her. She thought of what her mother had told her to do in situations like this one. Drive to the nearest police station or call 911. Those things were not options today.

The old highway was coming up fast. Her breathing quickened and her hands tensed around the wheel as she slowed in preparation of taking the turn. She took in more details about the car as she glanced at the mirror again, GTO spelled out in silver letters on the grille, exhaust ports on the hood that looked like the eyes of a coiled serpent, awaiting the right moment to strike.

She turned right onto the highway and sped up to reach the posted 55 MPH limit.

She looked at the rearview mirror.

The junker had turned in the same direction and was racing to catch up to her, its engine blatting like an enraged monster.

She grimaced.

Fuck.

The old highway was four lanes across, two lanes going in each direction.

At first Chelsea kept the speed of the Taurus just above the limit in the interest of adhering to the plan. Unfortunately, the plan hadn't taken into account the possibility of harassment by a deranged motorist. The junked-out GTO continued to stay right on her bumper, the driver revving the engine whenever possible while occasionally doing that unhinged swerving thing again.

She made a sound of annoyance and squeezed the wheel even tighter.

Why can't you just leave me alone, you fucking asshole?

She glanced at the gun, stashed for now in the middle console. Until today she'd been nothing but repulsed by guns and she still mostly felt that way, but now she knew she could use one if necessary. She took one hand off the wheel for a moment and switched off the weapon's safety. She still hoped the idiot behind her would come to his senses, get in the other lane, and drive on by, but things did not seem to be trending in that direction.

The driver of the GTO honked his horn, making her flinch.

A stray and entirely unwelcome thought floated into her head. What if the guy in the junker wasn't just some random sleazoid predator? What if he was somehow connected to the other men who'd terrorized her today?

A road that would lead straight into the heart of Lakemoor was coming up in about another mile and a half, more secondhand knowledge relayed by Zach from their mother. Lake City Boulevard. Noreen Murphy had mentioned it for landmark purposes. Once they were beyond it, they wouldn't need to turn again for another fifteen miles, at which point they'd be nearly all the way back to their hometown.

The GTO was still right behind them when Chelsea saw the street sign. It didn't take her long to realize the person hidden behind the tinted windows of the junker would be staying with her instead of heading into the small city.

This was becoming more ominous by the moment. The only reason Chelsea wasn't convinced this was yet another of the men looking for her father was that the previous two had been much sneakier in their initial approach. She figured anyone else associated with those guys would be at least as stealthy. The more she thought about it, the clearer it seemed that her original hunch was correct. She'd drawn the attention of a random psycho.

She considered an abrupt swerve to the left to take the turn toward town, but she had only seconds left to make the decision. There'd be potential dangers no matter what she decided. A deranged impulsive stalker might be less apt to accost or assault her in an area with lots of people around, but a detour into the city would also increase their odds of running into representatives of local law enforcement.

She sighed in frustration as she drove past the turn for Lake City Boulevard. A sense of regretful longing tugged at her as she looked at her side-view mirror and saw the turning point receding into the distance. Second thoughts assailed her, but she tried her best to push them away because it was too late now.

Her course was set.

And the junked-out GTO was still right behind her.

She looked at it in the rearview mirror as she increased her speed. It wasn't just right behind her, it was closer than ever, so close their bumpers must be almost touching. Another shiver of dread rippled through her as she imagined the old muscle car ramming the Taurus from behind.

The old highway's four lanes narrowed to two after only another mile. There were no more buildings, just miles and miles of empty rural road ahead. The GTO's driver honked again and did the swerving thing, wilder than before. Chelsea wished her brother was in the seat next to her. Not because he'd have some brilliant, better idea about what to do, but because the psycho in the GTO probably wouldn't be bothering her at all if he'd seen her in the company of a guy. But there was little point in wishing for impossible things. Her brother was where he was for the duration, just as she was stuck behind the wheel until this was over.

She was essentially alone, cut off from any form of help, with just an invisible monster for company on a long and lonely road.

Chelsea increased her speed again, going faster than she'd dared since the start of this ordeal.

Then faster still.

Because the monster was roaring and racing to catch up.

ELEVEN

THE COMPARTMENT DIRECTLY BENEATH THE
trapdoor was large enough for Noreen to stand. This was the opening
to the tunnel, the place where Jonathan had excavated the most earth
in order to have enough room to work. He'd had to do all the construction work himself because he wanted to keep knowledge of the
tunnel's existence contained. Only the two of them would know
about it. It was painstaking work that took most of a year. She'd as-
sisted by helping remove all the displaced earth from the house.
There'd been a lot of sweaty, sleep-deprived nights of dragging numerous overstuffed extra-large trash bags through the house and out
to her husband's truck. Hundreds upon hundreds of bags. All of
which were later torn open and emptied of their contents at several
widely spread apart dispersal points.

There were occasional complications during the construction process. More than once, Jonathan had to change the direction of his
tunneling to circumvent large slabs of rock. The result was a far more
twisty passage than the roughly straight line he'd hoped for in the
beginning. He also had to be careful not to cut into buried gas lines
and other old underground piping.

The project went on for so long and was so work-intensive that
somewhere around the midpoint Noreen ventured the notion of

abandoning it, an idea Jonathan refused to even consider. They argued about it as more months slipped by with the finish line still seeming impossibly far away. Bitterly so on a few occasions.

But Jonathan was stubborn. And determined.

Then, finally, just shy of a year later, the tunnel was complete.

Noreen was relieved and her husband was buoyed by a sense of profound accomplishment. He proclaimed the tunnel their ultimate insurance plan, their sure-fire means of slipping away should the walls ever close in. But that was years and years ago and they'd never had to make use of the elaborate safeguard. A big part of her had sincerely believed it'd never be necessary.

Things had changed, obviously.

Now she was glad of the tunnel's existence, grateful for Jonathan's vision and all his tireless work back then. There was a good chance it might end up saving not only her life but the lives of her children.

Noreen heaved a big breath and began to move forward out of the opening compartment, hunching over as the passage in front of her narrowed. About ten feet in it narrowed again, this time to the approximate circumference of a standard large drainage pipe. She knew from her one previous trip all the way through the tunnel and back the circumference would remain the same from this point through to the end.

She went to her hands and knees and entered the narrower part. The large handbag dragged on the ground beneath her torso, hanging by its straps around her neck. This was the only way she could think of to carry it through the tunnel without having to repeatedly toss it in front of her several feet at a time. She was just glad the passage wasn't narrow enough to force her to squirm forward on her belly. Battery-powered lanterns dangled from hooks embedded in support beams at regular intervals. She pushed the power buttons as she arrived at each one, brightly lighting the way forward. Only one lantern failed to power on, but it was okay because the faint light emanating from the previous lantern allowed her to see just well enough to reach the next location without difficulty.

Regular humans, if there'd been any who knew what she was, would probably expect her to see as easily in the dark as in daylight. An assumption based on what they knew of the preternaturally heightened senses of vampires from movies and books. And it was true there were vampires like that, a different species of blood-dependent human-like creatures. They were called nightsiders and were very much like the storybook creatures humans thought of when they thought about vampires. Because of their nocturnal nature, they did not often attempt to integrate themselves into normal human society the way daywalkers often did. They lived more savage lives in general. Some were almost feral. Noreen had carried on a brief but torrid affair with a nightsider several months after Jonathan had turned her. It'd been a kind of rebellion, a means of punishing him for taking her humanity without her consent. It'd also been one of the most simultaneously exhilarating and frightening experiences of her entire life.

As she came around a bend in the tunnel and powered on yet another lantern, she spied a pair of eyes gleaming in the light. She tensed for a moment, then realized the glowing eyes were too small and low to the ground to denote the presence of a creature worth fearing. The rat's whiskers twitched as she came closer, the rodent standing its ground until she was within a few feet, at which point it turned in a circle before scurrying off in the opposite direction.

The brief pause caused another flare of anxiety. She didn't like feeling like she wasn't in full control of any situation involving the safety of her kids, and in this case, at least for the time being, she had no control whatsoever. Nor would she be able to start doing anything about it until she was out of the tunnel. She willed herself to move faster, scurrying forward on her hands and knees with as much speed as she could generate in such cramped quarters, which was not inconsiderable. In addition to the physical boost she'd received from all the blood she'd consumed, she was also driven by nearly equal measures of fear and raw anger. It'd been years since she'd felt so fueled by primitive emotion.

She judged she was roughly two-thirds of the way to her destination when she was again forced to stop. If she'd simply run into another rat or other small creature, she would have ignored it and kept moving, but in this case she was shocked into temporary stillness. This happened as she was going around yet another curve in the passage, the bend obscuring the presence of the obstruction until she was nearly right up on it. She reached out to stab the power button on another lantern at the same time and that was when she saw it.

The corpse.

She gaped at it for several moments, unable to comprehend what she was seeing. Her mind reeled in disbelief because she knew there was only one person who could have stashed a corpse in the tunnel.

Jonathan.

After staring at it for at least another full minute, Noreen reached back and lifted the lantern she'd just powered on off its hook. She held it in front of her as she moved forward again to examine the body in the bright light. The corpse was mummified after an extended time of being sealed inside the tunnel. How long exactly it'd been in this place was hard to say, but she guessed it had to have been at least a year.

In other words, right around the time her husband took off.

Noreen's anger spiked yet again.

The corpse was female, judging from the long hair, jewelry, and clothing. New levels of astonishment kept coming at her in waves. She and Jonathan had spent nearly two decades committed to living as regular suburban people rather than as predators. They had a reliable source for blood and not once in all that time had their supply of it dipped below the level of plentiful. There was no need to hunt and drain blood from unwilling victims. It was the right way to live, the *best* way for the well-being of their family. They'd always been in full agreement on that count.

Or so she'd thought.

She shook with rage as she imagined what must have happened.

Her husband fell victim to the same malaise that affected so many human men after years of comfortable domestic tranquility. He grew restless, became nostalgic for the wild glory days of his youth. A craving for what he hadn't tasted in so long became harder and harder to resist, tormenting him with the forbidden joys of temptation until he succumbed. Then, like a long-term sober alcoholic finally relapsing, he realized just one fresh taste of that glorious nectar could never be nearly enough.

So he abandoned his family and returned to his former life. He was probably on the prowl somewhere out there right now, endeavoring to seduce some unsuspecting human female. She wondered if he'd fucked this one before taking all her blood.

Probably.

She tried telling herself this was only speculation, a worst-case scenario conjured by a mind already inclined toward suspicion. The body wasn't necessarily proof of anything other than he'd murdered someone, perhaps for reasons having nothing to do with what she was thinking.

But she didn't really believe that. Not for one second. All the elements fit together too perfectly. Her husband had strayed, betraying her faith in their bond. He'd embraced anew the darkest aspects of his vampiric nature, choosing a life of outlaw predation over the simple security of work and family. Noreen no longer felt the slightest trace of uncertainty regarding what she'd do when she was finally reunited with her husband.

I'm going to kill you, Jonathan. And I'm going to make you suffer.

Noreen unhooked the silver heart necklace the corpse wore around its withered neck and removed it. She dropped the necklace in her handbag and felt a smile of anticipation curve her lips. She would show Jonathan the necklace when she saw him. He would remember it, she had no doubt. Every luscious detail of the moment he gave in to his deepest desires would be etched vividly into his memory forever. She couldn't wait to see the look on his face the moment she placed it in his hand.

The look he showed her right before he finally realized just how badly he'd fucked up.

And how much he'd underestimated her.

Noreen maneuvered her way around the body and within a few more seconds had resumed her previous fevered pace. She moved with such speed this time that she occasionally bounced off the sides of the tunnel, but she barely noted these minor collisions. More than once she shot right by lanterns without hitting their power buttons, such was her hurry. Not even negotiating those stretches of nearly total darkness slowed her.

At long last, she entered the final stretch of the tunnel, something she knew because its circumference had widened again. She reached out and stabbed the power button on the final lantern, lighting up the large opening just ten feet in front of her.

She scrambled the rest of the way forward, walking hunched over at first and then rising to her full height as she entered a compartment identical to the one beneath the trapdoor back at her house.

A ladder in the compartment went straight up to another trapdoor.

Noreen started climbing.

TWELVE

THE CAR ROCKED AND SHUDDERED as the roaring GTO rammed into it from behind. This was it. The thing Chelsea had feared most, a direct assault while she was still sealed within the Taurus's illusory bubble of protection. Up to this point she'd held onto the belief she'd be okay if she could just stay ahead of the psycho until she could reach a safe place in her hometown. Somewhere public with lots of people around.

It was a scheme she'd been tempted to try in Lakemoor, but she'd opted against it because they were still so close to the scene of the shooting. There were undoubtedly cops looking for them on their home turf as well, albeit for different reasons, at least for now. That was likely to change soon enough. A connection would eventually be made between the report of missing kids and the deadly incident at the convenience store. Then those hometown cops wouldn't merely be searching for them out of concern for their safety.

Chelsea fought hard to hold onto the wheel as the GTO slammed into her rear bumper a second time. The Taurus swerved and straddled the yellow divider line. It kept drifting farther into the opposite lane until she was finally able to grip the wheel firmly enough to bring the car back across the line. She grimaced as she glanced at the speedometer and saw she was now going a hair under 70 MPH, which was a normal speed on the interstate, even kind of slow along some stretches. On this long stretch of winding rural highway filled with blind curves and steep dips and rises, it was dangerous, verging on suicidal. Even without some maniac pursuing her, driving through here at this speed would be risky in the extreme. Her heart felt like it was going a million miles an hour as she contemplated the likelihood of a fatal accident.

She could only imagine what Zach was going through in the trunk. He was being bounced around in the dark, clueless to the true nature of their current predicament. More than once she'd heard a muffled shout or cry from that direction. He had to be at least as scared shit-less as she felt, which was an already highly elevated level of scared shitless. There were of course things he *did* already know, like that they were fleeing from someone pursuing them with an unusual level of extreme aggression. It was possible he believed his sister was en-gaged in a high-speed chase with the Lakemoor police, an idea that would have seemed the height of absurdity a short while ago.

Not so much now.

Her gaze returned to the gun wedged in the middle console as the Taurus went up and over another steep hill. An idea flashed through her head. A crazy one that might just get them killed, but she didn't know how many more hits the Taurus could take from the GTO be-fore she lost control and went spinning off into the woods. There were still several miles remaining between her current position on the highway and the point where she was supposed to turn again. She was convinced she wouldn't be able to make it that far without doing something about their unknown adversary.

A total of two cars had passed them heading in the opposite di-rection the whole time they'd been on the two-lane stretch of high-way. She'd caught clear but fleeting glimpses of the wide-eyed looks of alarm from the drivers of those vehicles. The traffic was minimal but not non-existent. What she had in mind would not be without potential risk to other motorists, but anyone traveling along this road was already at risk of great bodily harm from the dangerously speed-ing vehicles.

Fuck it.

The instant she took the Taurus around another swooping curve and saw a relatively straight stretch of road ahead with no oncoming traffic, Chelsea abruptly swerved fully into the opposite lane and stomped on the brake. As she'd hoped, the maneuver took the driver of the GTO by surprise. The other car flew on by and was at least twenty feet away before it too came to a screeching halt. After idling for a few seconds, the other car's engine rumbled as it began to roll backward. Chelsea's heart was pounding harder than ever as she lowered the Taurus's driver-side window. She then set the brake, grabbed the gun, threw the door open, and hurled herself out of the car. Her hands trembled as she stood behind the open door and aimed the weapon at the slowly approaching rear end of the GTO.

It kept coming.

Either the psychopathic driver hadn't seen the gun yet or he was too smugly arrogant to ever believe a little thing like her would have the guts to use it. If he'd been at that convenience store a little while ago, he might have had a different opinion.

Chelsea waited until the GTO drew to within ten feet of her position.

Until she was sure she'd either have to do this or become a victim.

Another couple feet closer.

She grimaced as she squeezed the trigger.

And then squeezed it again and again, the bullets blowing through the windows and pocking the body of the vehicle. Five or six shots. Maybe seven. She lost count. BAM-BAM-BAM. So loud and percussive, her hands shaking as she struggled to hold onto the gun.

Chelsea heaved a breath as the GTO came to a full stop only a few feet away from the Taurus. Her hands continued to shake as she kept the gun trained on it, waiting for signs of life or counterattack. She figured odds were good an aggro male in an obnoxious ride like the junked-out GTO would have a gun in his glove box. He could be reaching for it even now.

She waited.

And waited.

No counterattack materialized.

She thought maybe the driver was already dead, one of her bullets having inflicted a fatal wound. A lucky headshot, perhaps. Then the driver shifted gears and began to drive away. Something was wrong, though, because the muscle car moved slowly while drifting toward the shoulder of the road. Then it was off the shoulder of the road and in the ditch. She kept staring at the GTO, waiting for the driver-side door to swing open, no doubt with a loud squeal of ancient hinges.

But it didn't happen.

She heard the rising buzz of an engine. Some other motorist

would be here within moments, a realization that shocked her out of her frozen pose. She jumped back in the Taurus, dumped the gun on the passenger seat, and closed the door. Her brother was yelling from the trunk, the hysterical sounds of his distress reaching a volume that allowed her to hear nearly every word clearly. She wished she had time to let him out and join her up front, but that engine buzz was getting louder by the millisecond.

Chelsea called out a few terse words of reassurance. Then she put the Taurus in gear and resumed the journey back toward their hometown at a saner speed, though she continued to sweat and breathe heavily for several more minutes. At one point she looked at the rearview mirror and noticed a strange thing.

She was smiling.

Yet another monster had come for her and once again it was she who'd been left standing at the end. *Not* the monster.

The smile stayed with her all the way back to town.

THIRTEEN

THE TRAPDOOR AT THIS END of the tunnel could only be unlatched and opened using a lever mechanism attached to its underside. Noreen pulled at the lever's handle and encountered some resistance, which was hardly surprising after so long a period of disuse, but her blood-augmented strength negated any difficulty. The latch disengaged with one more hard tug at the handle.

Noreen moved another step up the ladder as she pushed at the underside of the trapdoor. Another small bit of extra exertion was required to make it raise up high enough for her to poke her head through the opening. The top of the door was covered in a thin layer of dirt. Some of it spilled over the edges and into the tunnel opening as she pushed the door up a little higher. She took a look around and couldn't make out much of anything. The crawlspace beneath the house at 112 McGregor Street was cloaked in blackness. Memory told her the small sliding door leading out of the tight space was a short distance away in relative terms, but she wasn't keen on fumbling around in the dark in search of it.

She sighed and went back down the ladder, wishing she'd had the foresight to snag that last lantern in the tunnel in the first place. After retrieving it, she returned to the compartment beneath the trapdoor and again scaled the ladder. The door opened more easily this time.

She was still on the ladder, having climbed up just high enough for another look around. Raising the lantern, this time she clearly discerned a cramped space with a ceiling that couldn't be more than three feet above ground level. She also saw lots of spider webs, one of which was nearby with a disconcertingly large yellow and black spider lounging in its center.

Hoping not to startle the large creepy crawler into sudden fast-scuttling movement, she pushed at the trapdoor's underside again with exquisite slowness, moving up the ladder one cautious step at a time. She leaned through the opening and set the lantern and her purse on the ground a few feet away, crawled out, and gently lowered the trapdoor back into place. The whole time she was doing this, she kept a wary eye on the freakishly large spider, unsure of what she'd do if it were to come scuttling straight at her. It was kind of funny, a deadly supernatural creature being afraid of spiders, but it was primal instinct left over from her human days and she simply couldn't help it.

After grabbing her purse, she began crawling awkwardly in the direction of the door leading out of the crawlspace. The lantern was giving off enough light to leave it where it was. In addition, faint light was visible at the edges of the little sliding door, outlining its rectangular shape.

She knew the door opened into the backyard of the residence and could only hope no one was out there when she came squirming out, although a part of her found the idea amusing. Ordinary people minding their business on their own property, relaxing, enjoying the sunshine, when a naked woman covered in blood and dirt popped up out of nowhere. Less amusing was the knowledge of what she'd have to do if she did run into anyone out there.

She arrived at the door and spent a minute listening carefully for sounds of human activity from the yard.

Nothing.

She tried sliding the inner half of the door open and yet again encountered resistance. It took her a moment to realize this was because it was latched from the outside, which meant she'd have to break it open. This would result in an unavoidable burst of noise, a cracking and splintering of wood. Whether it'd be loud enough for anyone inside the house to hear, she did not know. Not that it mattered. She couldn't stay hidden away in the crawlspace forever.

Bracing her hands against the door, she began to push. At first the sound of wood splintering was faint, no louder than the creaking caused by footsteps on an old staircase. Then, as she increased the pressure by slow increments, the creaking gave way to sharp cracks. She cringed because it was a bit louder even than she'd expected, but she kept at it for the same reason she'd started, she had no choice. The door split fully apart with the loudest crack yet and she quickly scurried through the opening into the backyard.

She raised up on her knees and scanned her surroundings. As she'd hoped, there was no one in the yard, which was surrounded by a high wooden privacy fence. To her left, she saw a deck with a grill and lounge chairs. It looked much like the deck behind her own house, complete with the same type of French doors leading into the house. An unexpected pang of loss and nostalgia pierced her heart at the sight of it, bringing another unwelcome flood of good time memories from the days before Jonathan had betrayed them all.

There was no one on the deck.

Until about one second after Noreen got fully to her feet and sighed in relief at no longer being in cramped and unpleasant underground spaces. It was at that point one of the French doors opened and a pretty young woman in a blue sundress with white polka dots stepped out onto the deck. She had a hardcover book tucked under her arm and was carrying a tall glass filled with what might have been tea. The one thing Noreen noticed in that last split-second before the woman spotted her was how happy she looked. The smile that curved her lush lips was the kind some women wore when they were either harboring a secret source of joy or had just experienced a mind-melting orgasm.

It was a look of perfect contentment.

The beautiful smile vanished the instant she locked eyes with the naked, blood-covered woman in her backyard. Her mouth dropped open and the glass slipped from her fingers, tipping over as it hit the deck and spilling out the tea at her feet. The look on her face was one of utter stupefaction, a complete, albeit temporary, inability to comprehend what she was seeing.

Then a subtle shift occurred, a twitch of her features that signaled reality kicking in again. She dropped the book and turned toward the French doors. Another person might have screamed, demanding that Noreen immediately get off her property. This woman was smarter than that, and far more intuitive. One moment in Noreen's presence was all she'd needed to sense one thing with perfect clarity.

Danger.

The kind that couldn't be reasoned with or negated with threats.

She moved fast, her hand landing on a door handle barely a second later.

Noreen was faster.

She caught up to the woman before she could get the door fully open, wrapping her up in her arms and holding her still as easily as she'd hold a newborn kitten. Her mouth found the side of the woman's slender neck and opened wide, allowing her to feel the presence of her elongating fangs. The woman trembled, whimpering as her bladder voided and urine began to run down her legs, the acrid scent causing Noreen's nose to twitch as she shuddered with pleasure.

She'd almost forgotten what it was like to experience the helpless fear of a victim, what an intoxicatingly intimate thing it could be. The feeling was different from what she'd experienced with the one-eyed man. That'd been an act of savage vengeance, a brutal and primal thing. She'd been almost like a mindless animal while it was happening. This time her mind and senses were fully engaged, savoring every sweet nuance. Her nipples stiffened as she became intensely aroused, the way she always had in the old days in the moments right before her fangs sank into tender flesh and she tasted that first divine spurt of fresh blood entering her mouth.

No.

This was not what she wanted.

She had worked so hard for so many years to suppress her predatory instincts. To allow them to assume full rein again so easily would mean she'd failed. Once upon a time, she'd been a monster, a destroyer of innocence, and she'd rejected that in favor of recommitting herself to the basic tenets of human decency and morality. Never mind that she was no longer truly human. Never mind that in the beginning she'd done it solely for the sake of staying safe and hidden. Over time she'd become a genuinely good person again, or so she'd believed, and now she was on the verge of flushing all that work down the drain. One act of enraged bloodletting was all it'd taken to reawaken that inner predator and bring her to the very brink of losing all control.

Taking her mouth away from the woman's neck required a supreme act of concentrated will, one she wasn't sure would succeed. Having allowed things to reach this point, she knew the vampiric urge could still easily result in an impulse puncture. If that happened, the woman wrapped so tightly in her arms would be doomed. Even one drop of hot blood on her tongue would trigger an irresistible and deadly response.

She pressed her mouth against the woman's ear. "Stop crying. Stop begging. Those things make it harder to let you go. So stop."

The woman sniffled. "Please don't hurt me."

Her voice was a fragile whisper, the rapid, fluttery beating of her heart such an exquisitely vulnerable thing.

Noreen's grip on the woman tightened. "What did I say about not begging? You're practically asking me to kill you."

"I'm sorry."

The woman was such a delicate little flower. Taking her apart like one would unquestionably be the single most intensely pleasurable thing she'd experienced in a long time. The temptation to give in to these urges was growing, becoming stronger with every second that passed with the woman still wrapped in her arms.

No. You can't.

But she could. It would be so easy.

She summoned another massive effort of will and whispered into the woman's ear again. "You listen to me, little flower, if you want to live. Is there anyone else in the house? Tell the truth or you'll suffer. Lying to protect a loved one won't work out well for you or them."

The woman sniffled and let out a shuddery breath. "It's just me here right now. That's the truth, I swear. My husband's out of town on business and my kids are spending a week with their grandparents in Arkansas."

Noreen believed her. She'd forgotten how easy it was to discern the truth from lies when holding a piece of helpless prey in her grip. The physiological symptoms were unmistakable.

She loosened her grip on the woman slightly but did not release her. "How fortunate for everyone's sake, including mine. Slaughtering an entire family would not have been my preference."

The woman was still trembling and crying.

It felt so fucking good.

"A-are you going to . . . hurt me?"

Noreen laughed softly. "I'm trying so hard not to, flower. You have no idea. What's your name?"

"A-Amelia."

"Hmm. I like that. It suits you. A beautiful name for a beautiful flower."

The woman's only response to that was another whimper.

Noreen slowly disengaged herself from the woman but kept a hand on her waist. "We're going inside now, Amelia. You must be careful not to make any sudden moves or do anything else stupid. In fact, don't do anything I don't explicitly tell you to do. Understood?"

Amelia nodded. "Yes."

Noreen detected no subterfuge in the single syllable.

"You may yet live to see another day, flower. I hope so. But before that's decided, I'll need to spend some time in your home. Not too long, I hope, but you'll need to be very brave for a while."

And on that note, they entered the house.

FOURTEEN

ZACH SPENT AROUND HALF AN hour confined in the trunk of the Taurus, but it felt much longer than that. He'd known there might be some tense moments along the way and had tried to brace himself for that, but nothing could have prepared him for what actually transpired. The ordeal was made exponentially worse by his inability to see what was happening. His imagination ran wild. It didn't take a genius to figure out they were being aggressively pursued during one long stretch of his confinement, but were the pursuers cops or more of those people looking for their father?

There was no way to know.

Things kept getting scarier and more fucked up. The worst of it was when the Taurus came to a sudden, fishtailing stop and the shooting started.

He'd nearly wet himself.

For a few grief-stricken moments, he'd been convinced his sister was lying dead in the street, leaking blood from multiple holes in her slender torso. He'd felt an anguished scream rising up from deep inside him, but then someone—he could only hope and assume it was his sister—got back in the Taurus and started driving again. He yelled and kicked at the lid of the trunk. The identity of the person behind the wheel was confirmed when Chelsea responded with a shouted admonishment about chilling out.

There was no more drama after that, aside from the anxiety gnawing away at his nerves for the duration of the ride. Chilling out was not a real option. They'd survived yet another crisis, but how long would it be before another one came along? How long could their luck possibly hold out?

He was pondering that very thing for perhaps the thousandth time when the Taurus, which had been traveling at a significantly slower speed the last few minutes, slowed further still and changed directions a couple more brief times before coming to a stop. He heard Chelsea put the car in park and engage the brake. Then the engine cut off and door hinges squeaked as she got out. Seconds later, a key rattled in the trunk's lock. Then he was blinking against the sudden intrusion of bright sunlight as the lid came open.

Zach squinted at his sister. "What the actual fuck was up with all that *Fast & Furious* bullshit?"

She reached in and grabbed him by the hand. "No time. We gotta move. Come on."

He climbed out of the trunk and took a look around.

The Taurus was parked at a sideways angle across two parking spaces at the side of what appeared to be an abandoned gas station, the back end pointed away from the street. There was a large covered area and a few elevated slabs of concrete once occupied by pumps that must have been removed years ago. The patches of grass growing up here and there through cracks in the faded asphalt imbued the place with an eerie post-apocalyptic feel. Something about what he was seeing sparked a sense of familiarity, but it took him a moment to figure out why.

Chelsea had succeeded in returning them to their hometown. Back in his junior high days, the bus he rode to school drove by this spot every day. He'd barely taken note of it back then, but he remembered the old gas station had been abandoned even then. They were on the opposite side of town from the neighborhood where they'd grown up. The part of town where the storage unit their mother had told him about prior to their departure from Lakemoor was located. Just a few blocks down the street from where they stood now, in fact.

Zach grunted. "You did it."

Chelsea nodded as she shouldered his backpack and slammed the trunk lid down. "Yeah. Come on."

She started walking away from the Taurus without waiting for a response, heading straight for the road.

He hurried to catch up, having to put a serious spring in his step. She was moving fast. He understood the urgency but felt a bit put off by her abrupt manner. They turned to the right as they reached the road and started walking along the shoulder. There was no sidewalk. Traffic passed in both directions. Not a lot, but a steady stream. No one seemed to take any special notice of them, but Chelsea glanced back once and told him to keep his head down. Though her attitude rankled him, he understood the wisdom of the advice and endeavored to keep his face turned away from the street every time a vehicle passed by.

Once, during a brief lull in traffic, he asked her if he could have his backpack back.

She shook her head without glancing back at him that time. "No."

The response made him frown. "Why not?"

She sighed but maintained her fast pace. "Because the gun is in the backpack. It's better if I have it."

That made his frown deepen. "Why's that?"

"Because we already know I have the nerve to use it."

Whereas Zach had not yet proven himself on that level, was the unspoken part of that thought.

Once again, it rankled him a little, but he couldn't really argue, either.

She was only stating an absolute fact.

As they continued moving up the street at the same rapid clip, he kept a constant eye out for police cruisers. One hadn't appeared yet, but they couldn't let their guard down. An active attempt to track them down was undoubtedly well underway. For all they knew, their faces might already have appeared on local television screens. *Anybody* might recognize them at any moment and call in the sighting. Seen in that light, Chelsea's escalated air of no-nonsense ultra-urgency was the only sensible mindset. He quickened his step until he was walking right alongside her.

He glanced at her, wishing again to ask her about what had happened out there on the road, but her look of intense concentration dissuaded him. She was doing an amazing impersonation of a genuine badass, but he sensed her terror lurking right beneath the surface. He saw it in the strained set of her features and in the way her eyes kept darting nervously around. A brotherly urge to tell her everything was going to be okay made his mouth open, but the words did not emerge.

Mostly he didn't want to say that and have it turn out to be a lie. That was a real possibility and it would remain so as long they were out in the open like this.

The tensest moments of their journey came when they arrived at an intersection where they had to stop and watch traffic until the crossing light came on. Chelsea was off and moving faster than ever the instant the glowing white letters that spelled out WALK appeared. Zach again hurried to match her pace, his heart pounding by the time they reached the other side.

He had no real expectations of being able to outrun the police had a cruiser passed by during those helpless moments of waiting, but their mother had urged them to do whatever they could to avoid apprehension. The words "at all costs" had been used. That seemed extreme given they were just kids trying to do what felt like impossible things.

A part of him was still clinging to a desperate belief that all the legally questionable things they'd done could be explained away. They'd been swept up in a situation they didn't understand. They had legitimate cause to fear for their lives. The dead man they'd left behind at the gas station had come at Chelsea with a shotgun.

The cops could be made to understand those things. He sincerely believed that.

It didn't matter.

Willing surrender to the authorities would be a betrayal of their mother's wishes and therefore it couldn't happen. Chelsea would never go along with it, for one thing. At this moment in time, Zach's primary loyalty was to his sister, and he intended to see this nightmarish odyssey through to the end with her, wherever it led.

The storage facility came into view two more blocks down the street, but they were on the wrong side of the road. After waiting for traffic to clear, they raced over to the other side, arriving just ahead of a speeding pickup truck that honked at them. Zach restrained an impulse to wave a middle finger, knowing yet another confrontation could lead to disastrous consequences.

Barely more than a minute later, they were walking up the paved drive toward the facility's gated entrance.

Chelsea exhaled heavily. "We made it."

It was the first thing she'd said to him since denying his request for the backpack.

A tentative half-smile trembled at the edges of her mouth.

Zach touched her arm. "We're gonna be okay."

She wiped her eyes and said, "I hope so."

They continued up the driveway, bypassing an office building with a small parking lot surrounded by a tall wrought-iron fence. Zach grimaced as he kept walking and tried not to stare at the building. He half-expected some belligerent person to come out of the building to demand an explanation for their presence. That didn't happen, but his fear of imminent confrontation remained even as they moved past the building, arriving at a keypad mounted on a pole near the gate.

Zach punched in the code Noreen Murphy made him memorize, and they hurried on into the facility as the gate began to slide open.

The layout of the place was almost like that of a little town or neighborhood, with numerous long rows of a larger sized unit sectioned off from rows of smaller units. There were two rows of deluxe units Zach thought of as the mansions of the maze-like facility. His parents had rented one of the standard-sized units at some unknown point in the past and had been paying for it every month for, well, a long time, something Zach and Chelsea had been unaware of until today.

That by itself was weird enough.

Even weirder, they hadn't rented the unit using their real names. This was just one of a bewildering series of unexplained revelations that had come to light during the frantic phone conversation with their mother. Noreen had shared the information about the false rental identity in case they were confronted by anyone employed by the facility. In such an eventuality, they were to explain they'd been authorized by Margaret Lancaster (aka Noreen Murphy) to access unit 612 on an emergency basis in order to retrieve important documents.

As cover stories went, it wasn't the most convincing Zach had ever heard. Why would his mother keep documents that important in a storage unit instead of on file with her lawyer? He couldn't see how it would hold up to any serious scrutiny. In the end, it hadn't mattered, because they'd walked on in without encountering anyone who worked at the place.

As they moved through the facility, they spotted a couple of cars parked in the spaces between rows of units, presumably belonging to other people who'd rented space here. The garage-like doors of these units were standing open, the visitors out of sight.

The lack of eyes on them came as a relief, but it was tempered by the knowledge that someone could pop out of one of those open units at any moment and spot them. Maybe even recognize them. Even though they were off the street, the sense of urgency that had gripped the siblings remained in place and kept them moving at a fast pace.

At last they arrived at the row of units where 612 was located. A small iota of tension leaked out of Zach's body as they turned down the row and saw no cars. By unspoken agreement, they abandoned their fast walking pace and ran the rest of the way. The hasp lock on the door was secured with a padlock, which fortunately was the kind that opened with a combination instead of a key. Of the many things his mother had told him during that last conversation, the combination had been the easiest to remember.

It was their parents' wedding anniversary.

He dialed in the combination and the lock came easily open when he pulled on it, removing it from the hasp. As soon as he'd done that, Chelsea grabbed hold of the door handle and heaved the door upward with a loud grunt of exertion. The sound of the door ratcheting upward was louder than Zach cared for, making him grimace as he glanced back the way they'd come.

There was still no one in the vicinity.

A light switch was on the wall just inside the door.

Chelsea flipped it on and fluorescent lights on the ceiling flickered to life, brightly illuminating the interior of the unit after a few seconds. Brother and sister stood at the front of the unit, gazing at its contents in silence for several moments.

Then they glanced at each other.

Chelsea said, "Holy shit."

Zach nodded. "Yeah."

Another brief period of total silence ensued.

Then Chelsea shivered and said, "Jesus. Who are Mom and Dad? *What* are they?"

These were good questions.

Zach, unfortunately, had no answers for them.

They entered the unit and pulled the door down.

FIFTEEN

AMELIA'S HOUSE WAS IMMACULATE ON the inside, without a speck of dirt or dust anywhere in sight. The appliances in the kitchen gleamed like they were brand new from the showroom. All the furniture was of the highest quality, luxuriously plush and comfy chairs and sofas, a long and gleaming mahogany table in the large dining room that looked fit for entertaining royalty. The wall-mounted television in the living room was the biggest she'd ever seen in a personal residence. The television in the den of chez Murphy had a 70-inch screen, but this one was significantly larger. Noreen hadn't realized televisions with screens this size were even sold at the retail level. It looked like something that should be at a football stadium instead of in someone's home.

This was some serious wealth on display.

She'd never closely interrogated Jonathan regarding the spot he'd chosen for the tunnel's ultimate point of egress. All he'd ever told her was that the crawlspace beneath the house would make an ideal intermediary hiding place should an emergency escape ever become necessary. She'd seen the logic in that and hadn't pursued the matter further.

But now she wondered.

Amelia was such a luscious little thing, almost doll-like in her delicate beauty. There was a time when Noreen had truly believed Jonathan was no longer interested in other women, at least not in a serious way. They'd both left all that behind after deciding to transition to the normie life. All the meaningless little flings vampires who were active hunters always had, most of which were dalliances with mortals whose lives they'd later take. It'd all been consigned to the past, changed out for a safer existence.

They were committed to each other. To their family.

To their new purpose together.

Noreen had believed in that shared purpose wholeheartedly right up to the day Jonathan disappeared.

What if he'd never genuinely shared her conviction? What if, for him, it'd never been anything more than an act all along? The thought made her tremble with fury because she realized she was already most of the way down the road to believing it.

What if there'd been more to his thinking in selecting the tunnel's egress spot than mere practicality?

At a rough guess, Amelia was somewhere in her mid-thirties. It was possible she'd lived in this place long enough to coincide with the construction of the tunnel. Maybe Jonathan had been obsessed with her. She certainly possessed the kind of beauty that engendered feelings of obsession. Perhaps he'd planned to take her as his next victim or lover. Or both.

Maybe he already had.

Noreen made Amelia walk ahead of her as they climbed the stairs to the second floor. Her little polka-dotted blue dress was almost unbearably cute, like the kind of thing an idealized housewife in a '50s sitcom would wear. Even after the brief struggle on the deck out back, her hair had an ultra-stylish fresh-from-the-salon look. Her every movement was so feminine and graceful, which was amazing given the stress she must be feeling.

Noreen scowled as they reached the top of the stairs.

Amelia glanced over her shoulder at her as they continued down the upstairs hallway, her pretty features crumpled in a look of worry. "You really don't need to hurt me. I'll do anything you say."

Noreen laughed. "Of course you will."

They entered the master bedroom through an open door at the end of the hallway. The centerpiece of the room was a large sleigh-style bed with an ornate wooden headboard and footboard.

Noreen placed a hand at the small of Amelia's back and guided her over to the side of the bed, where she lifted the woman off the floor and set her down on the edge.

Amelia's eyes widened at this display of unnatural strength. "What . . . what are you?"

Noreen smiled. "Come on, Amelia. You felt my fangs. You already know."

Fear flickered in the woman's expression. "You're a vampire."

Noreen nodded, her smile starting to fade. "Yes. And it's interesting how automatically you say that, without a trace of skepticism. Without even questioning how I'm functioning in daylight. People who only know the old cliches, that's usually the first thing they ask." She paused a moment, her eyes boring into Amelia. "Sometimes it's the last thing they ever say."

Amelia trembled. "You don't have to hurt me."

Noreen put a hand on her throat. "You keep saying that. I fucking know I don't *have* to hurt you, bitch." Her grip tightened, painfully compressing the woman's tender flesh. "But maybe I *want* to. I'm not the first vampire you've ever met, am I? Tell me the truth or you'll never take another breath."

She loosened her grip slightly.

Amelia whimpered. "No. I'm sorry."

Noreen sneered. "What are you apologizing for?"

Amelia only whimpered again.

Noreen felt she already knew the truth, but she needed to hear the woman say it. "Did you fuck Jonathan Murphy?"

The woman's chin had dropped toward her chest, but now she lifted her head again and met Noreen's steely gaze. "He forced himself on me the first time. He threatened me. Threatened my children. But . . ."

Noreen waited a moment before prompting her. "But . . . what?'

Amelia swallowed with difficulty, her eyes growing wet. "I fell in love with the things he could do to me. The things he could make me feel. Things no ordinary man could ever do."

Noreen let out a slow breath. "How many times?"

Amelia sniffled. "I lost count over the years."

Noreen's eyes blazed with rage.

Amelia squirmed in her grip. "I'm sorry. I—"

She couldn't speak after that because Noreen had clamped her hand too tightly around the woman's throat.

"I know it wasn't your fault, sweet little Amelia. You couldn't resist him. It wouldn't have been possible. You're only a sniveling little human. A pathetic and pliable little doll. Here's what you don't understand. He's my property. *Mine.* That means you have transgressed against me and that cannot stand."

She began to bend her fingers inward, her long red fingernails digging into the human's soft flesh. Noreen held the woman's terrified gaze, beginning to smile again as her nails pierced the flesh and blood began to flow. She did this slowly at first, drawing out the woman's pain and suffering, then with a roar of primal anger she finished it fast, tearing out her throat.

Noreen opened her mouth wide and pressed her face against the eruption of blood.

She drank deeply again, savoring every sweet drop, but this time she did not fully drain her victim because she wasn't yet finished with Amelia. Soon she relaxed her grip on the lifeless body and allowed it to slide to the blood-soaked carpet.

Then she went into the room's attached bathroom and turned on the shower.

SIXTEEN

AS HE EXPLORED THE INTERIOR of the storage unit, Zach's mind kept returning to a question Chelsea had asked upon first glimpsing its contents. Not the one about who their parents were because obviously the use of a false name gave rise to matters of identity confusion. They could no longer even be certain the names they'd always known their parents by were their real ones. If they'd used one set of false names, they might well have used others. This in itself was troubling. No, the question Zach kept returning to was the other one his sister had asked.

The one about *what* their parents were.

Because he was having tremendous difficulty thinking of any non-sinister explanation for why a pair of ostensibly ordinary married suburbanites would have a secret storage unit stocked with a vast array of weaponry and a silver Honda Accord that was probably a couple of decades old.

Among other, even stranger things.

They'd found the car unlocked with the key inserted halfway into the ignition slot. A check of the glove box revealed a registration under the name Bridget Robbins, which Zach could only assume was another false identity. Even stranger, the registration and the license plate were up to date. These things were all highly perplexing, but far more worrisome was the humming refrigerator filled with pouches of blood. Then there was the long black coffin resting on a table at the rear of the unit. Neither of them had worked up the nerve to open it thus far.

Chelsea popped open the Honda's trunk and started rooting around inside it while Zach examined the wall of weaponry. There were a lot of long guns on racks, ranging from simple hunting rifles and shotguns to the type of semi-automatic assault-style weapons currently favored by drooling maniacs with a vendetta all over the country. Lined up along the floor beneath the racks of long guns were multiple wooden crates filled with ammunition. On another table near the back were stacks of what appeared to be various types of handguns still in their retail packaging, along with still more crates of ammo stashed beneath the table.

The range of weapons on display was not limited to firearms. There were axes and machetes, swords and long, deadly-looking knives with thick, serrated blades suitable for eviscerating one's enemies on a medieval battlefield. One of the axes was massive and double-bladed. It looked designed for use by a giant.

A fucking mace was hanging from a hook.

Zach raised a tentative finger, touching the tip of it against one of the spikes protruding from the iron ball dangling from the chain attachment. He supposed he'd harbored some fragile hope the thing was a prop made of rubber, but the sharp point of the spike pierced his flesh instantly, drawing forth a small bead of blood and erasing all doubt regarding its authenticity.

He winced and popped the finger into his mouth, sucking on the blood.

"Holy shit!"

Zach flinched at his sister's loud exclamation.

He turned away from the wall of mass destruction and saw Chelsea standing at the back of the Accord. The trunk lid was open. She'd pulled something onto the lip of the trunk and was gawking at it with a wide-eyed look of awe and disbelief.

"What is it?"

Chelsea's gaze stayed on whatever had elicited the shocked reaction. "Come see."

Zach took his wounded fingertip from his mouth and wiped it on his pants as he walked over to the open trunk and took a look.

"Holy shit."

Chelsea nodded. "Yeah."

Propped on the lip of the trunk was an open canvas travel bag stuffed to bursting with banded stacks of cash.

Zach took one, inch-thick stack from the bag and riffled through it with his thumb. The bills were all hundreds. He glanced at the open bag and saw many more banded stacks of hundreds, as well as quite a few stacks of fifties and twenties. The bag was of the larger, longer style. He tried to do a rough estimate of how much cash it might contain and arrived at a general amount that boggled conception.

"There's gotta be at least a million dollars here."

Chelsea nodded again. "Maybe more. Maybe a *lot* more."

Zach peered into the trunk and saw another bag just like the one Chelsea had already opened. It looked equally overstuffed. He guessed they should probably open that one too, but it seemed likely to contain another massive shit-ton of cash. Also in the trunk was a large cardboard box with its flaps open. He pulled one of them back and saw dozens of burner phones in plastic clamshell packaging.

Chelsea looked at him. "Do you think the money is real? Maybe Mom and Dad are counterfeiters or con artists, something crazy like that."

Zach's brow furrowed and he made a contemplative noise as he thumbed through the same stack of bills again. "They sure as shit look real. Kind of older, but real." He took another pointed look around. "And I've got this feeling our parents aren't anything as mundane as ordinary con artists."

He peeled several bills from the stack he was holding and shoved them into one of his pockets.

"Zach!"

He glanced at her again, shrugging. "What? Let's be real, Chel, Mom and Dad didn't come by any of this honestly. I mean, how much money do you have on you? Any at all? I've only got a few bucks. Think about what happens if Mom doesn't show up. I won't be able to use my debit card again because it'd be traced. We won't get very far without taking some of this for ourselves. In fact . . ."

He peeled another several bills from the stack and shoved them in his pocket with the others, then tossed what was left back in the bag.

Chelsea chewed on her lower lip a moment, looking troubled. "Huh. You might have a point."

Then she grabbed the same stack Zach had already pilfered and peeled away several more bills for herself. After folding over the bills and tucking them inside her bra, she zipped up the bag, tossed it deeper into the trunk, and waved Zach out of the way so she could close the lid.

They were silent for a few moments after that, lost in their own thoughts.

Then Zach sighed. "So . . . Mom and Dad. Are they, like, spies or something?" His head turned toward the wall of weapons, his eyes going to the mace again. "Or revolutionaries, maybe? Part of some kind of weird organization of super ninja assassins? I mean . . ." He waved a hand at the wall. "If it's not something like that, then why all this? And what about the phones? That's definitely shady, right? On TV shows, spies and criminals use them once and throw them away."

Chelsea shrugged. "I don't know. This is all so strange. When would they have the time to be involved with super ninja revolutionary assassin stuff? It doesn't make any sense. Mom was always at home. Dad had his job and sometimes he went out of town on business, but never for crazy amounts of time. The job wasn't a lie. We visited the office enough to know that. They were both so . . . normal."

Zach nodded. "Yeah. Except . . . Dad's been gone a while now. The phrase 'mysterious circumstances' was pretty much invented for what happened to him."

The unexplained disappearance of their father had always been a deeply upsetting thing, but now it was troubling in ways they'd never imagined. Who knew how it related to what they'd discovered here today?

Chelsea grunted. "Well, what do we do now? Stay here until things quiet down?"

Zach shook his head. "Mom wants us to go to a cabin on Stillwater Lake, but we're supposed to wait for her to join us here first."

His sister's brow creased and she gnawed on her lower lip again, making fitful, fidgety gestures with her hands as she glanced first at the wall of weapons and then at the refrigerator. These were mannerisms her brother was well acquainted with, having grown up with her.

"Spit it out, Chel."

She had tears in her eyes when she looked at him. "Do we know we can trust Mom? Do we know if we *should*?"

Zach's answer to that question at any point prior to this moment would have been an automatic and emphatic *yes*. There'd never been anyone in the world he trusted and believed in more than his mother.

But now he wasn't so sure.

"What are you saying?"

She bounced on her toes a time or two, adrenaline and nerves beginning to overwhelm her. "I think maybe I'm a little afraid of her." She paused a moment. "Maybe more than a little."

Zach nodded.

The sentiment was one he wished he could reject, but he thought again of how his mother had acted since showing up seemingly out of nowhere to thwart the one-eyed man's insidious plans. It was as if someone had flipped a switch, instantly transforming her into an entirely different person. A person with a great capacity for ruthlessness, and one who did not shy away from deadly conflict.

Noreen Murphy had evidently had a *lot* to hide, all of it still wrapped in many layers of impenetrable mystery.

Chelsea opened the refrigerator again. "Here's what freaks me out the most. Other than hospitals, who needs that much fucking blood?"

Zach could see the inside of the fridge from where he stood leaning against the back of the car. The appliance was as overstuffed with plump blood bags as the travel bags were with cash. The shelves, drawers, and side slots were packed full of them. No space remained for anything else.

He laughed. "Vampires."

Chelsea showed him a look of confusion. "What?"

Zach shrugged, laughing again. "Obviously I'm not serious, but if vampires were a real thing, they'd want what's in that fridge. It'd probably be worth more to them than the money."

Chelsea frowned.

She glanced inside the fridge again, let go of the door handle, and trained her attention on the long black coffin.

Zach followed her gaze. "Um, no. Come on, Chel. The vampire thing was a joke. Mom's not a bloodsucker out of some cheesy old movie. Neither is Dad. They walk around in the daytime. There's no coffins at the house. I don't know why they have that thing here, but it's not because they're fucking vampires. Hell, there's probably just more guns or phones or whatever in it."

Chelsea's gaze was still on the coffin, a worried, contemplative look on her face. "Should we look inside it?"

The suggestion filled Zach with apprehension.

He believed fully in what he'd told his sister. They had many legitimate reasons to feel a deep paranoia regarding virtually every aspect of the situation, but that only meant they should remain vigilant about continuing to focus on what they knew to be real. Going off the deep end into fantastical theories about everything would be the opposite of helpful.

Vampires were creatures of myth. They didn't exist.

The only monsters in this world were those of the human variety.

The idea of opening the gothic-looking black coffin nonetheless triggered a queasy reaction in some primal part of his psyche.

Chelsea walked up to the coffin and glanced back at him. "Gonna help me with this?"

Zach shrugged, not wanting to cop to how spooked he felt. "Sure."

He approached the coffin and together they grasped the edge of the lid, grunting in exertion as they strained to lift it upward. It would not budge. They strained hard enough that the bottom of the coffin raised off the table by a fraction of an inch.

They gave up at the same time, huffing from the strain as they moved back a step and stared in consternation at the thing.

Chelsea pursed her lips. "Do you think it's nailed shut?"

Zach moved closer again, peering closely at the side of the lid. "I see no evidence of that."

"Maybe there's a lock?"

Zach ran his fingers along the edge of the lid at the bottom, about an inch of which protruded beyond the coffin's side. About a third of the way down, he encountered what felt like a small clasp or latch. He pushed at it and heard a loud metallic click.

Chelsea laughed.

Zach groaned in annoyance.

He tested the lid and was able to lift it higher with little effort.

Chelsea was still laughing.

Zach scowled. "Excuse me for not being skilled in the funereal arts or whatever the proper technical term is. I've never set foot in a funeral home. Never attended a funeral."

Chelsea's look of amusement faded, her expression turning thoughtful again. "Because we've never known anybody who died. Not until today."

She was right.

They'd never attended a service after the passing of an elder relative because they had no elder relatives, at least not as far as they were aware. Noreen and Jonathan Murphy both came from small families and had no surviving kin, or so they'd always claimed.

Zach lifted the lid higher.

A foul odor wafted from the interior of the coffin.

Chelsea gagged. "Oh, God, what is that awful smell?"

Instead of answering, Zach continued lifting the lid, then pushed it backward until the hinges at the back locked into place, holding it in an upright position. He then looked into the coffin and felt his guts clench again.

"Oh, fuck."

Chelsea moved closer and looked inside, immediately echoing her brother. "Oh, fuck."

Inside the coffin was a rotted corpse attired in a suit and tie. It'd not been inside the coffin for so long that it was down to only bones. There were still fleshy remains, blackened and withered with glimpses of the skeletal frame beneath visible here and there. Limp blond hair was still attached to the scalp.

Chelsea put a hand over her mouth and stepped back. "There's a fucking dead dude in there, Zach. What the fuck?"

Her voice trembled on the edge of hysteria.

Zach turned and looked at her. "Let's get the fuck out of here."

She nodded as tears began to spill down her cheeks. "Okay."

And just a short while later, after gathering some things they thought they might need, they did exactly that.

SEVENTEEN

AMELIA'S EYES FLUTTERED OPEN AND for a few moments she stared blearily up at the ceiling. Her slack features and glassy eyes gave her a dazed look, which was understandable for one newly returned from the realm beyond death. The dazed look slowly faded, replaced by a dawning awareness of restored consciousness.

She touched a hand to her throat, fingers probing for the ragged hole she knew should be there, focus returning to her expression as she realized it was gone. Her hand came away from her throat and she stared at fingers sticky with coagulating blood. There was a clear sense of mystified wonder in her expression. The blood she'd expected was present, but the wound was gone, erased as if it'd never existed.

Sitting up, she gasped when she saw Noreen seated in a chair in a corner of the room. "What have you done? I thought you killed me. Was it all a dream?"

Clad in a plush white bathrobe, Noreen sat on the edge of the chair and observed Amelia's process of vampiric rebirth with a mixture of amusement and clinical curiosity. The little housewife's confusion made her smile. It was fascinating to watch because it was like seeing a replay of what she'd gone through on the long-ago day when she lost her humanity.

"It wasn't a dream, sweet Amelia. I *did* kill you. But now I've brought you back."

A troubled look crossed Amelia's face as she again touched her throat, her fingers moving over the entire expanse of flesh, seeking additional tactile confirmation the wound really was gone.

She made eye contact with Noreen. "How?"

Noreen smirked. "Hello? I'm a vampire, remember? How do you think it happened? I killed you, but I didn't drain you. Then I fed you some of my blood. It's the standard way it's done, the interaction of vampiric blood and human blood. It's alchemy. Magic. Whatever you want to call it. Anyway, you're back. Aren't you happy?"

Amelia stared at her without speaking for a longish period, her expression suggesting an internal debate was occurring. Then she said, "I'm glad I'm not dead. But does this mean . . ."

Noreen nodded. "Yes. You're a vampire now. A daywalker, like me. But your transformation isn't complete. You'll need to feed within the first twenty-four hours to make it permanent."

"Feed?"

Another nod from Noreen. "Yes. You'll need to drink fresh human blood directly from the source, and a lot of it. Ideally, you'd fully drain your first victim."

Amelia grimaced. "I'll have to kill someone?"

"Yes."

"What if I can't do it?"

Noreen shrugged. "Then you will die. And not easily. It will be a protracted and ugly death. You'll feel pain like nothing you've ever experienced, like every nerve ending in your body is on fire constantly, and it will not stop until you're gone. Which can take weeks, by the way." She chuckled, her eyes glittering with dark amusement. "If you choose death by some alternative method, some more immediate means of suicide, just be aware you'll need to ensure your body is completely destroyed. It takes a lot to kill a daywalker. Decapitation works too but you'd need to find someone willing to chop off your head. Honestly, I wouldn't recommend that option either, as consciousness in the mind of a beheaded vampire endures far longer than you'd find pleasant."

Amelia was left stunned by this deluge of troublesome information, her mouth hung open as she stared at Noreen and struggled to make sense of her new reality. Then she swallowed and said, "I guess I have no choice."

"Because you don't want to suffer."

Amelia shook her head. "No."

Noreen smiled. "Understandable. I made the same choice years ago. But do not delude yourself about what this means. In order to survive and thrive, other people, *innocent* people, *will* have to suffer at your hands."

Tears welled in Amelia's eyes. "Why did you do this to me? How can I stay with my family without endangering them?"

Noreen rose from the chair and removed the bathrobe, allowing it to fall to the floor. The little black dress she'd removed from the closet at her house was on a hanger hooked over the top of the bathroom door. She took it off the hanger and pulled it on over her head, tugging at it and smoothing the fabric down, pleased to find that it fit as well as it had the last time she'd worn it. That closet in the guest bedroom was full of relics from long ago. It might have been decades since she'd last donned this particular dress.

She'd given some thought to wearing something from Amelia's wardrobe instead, but the garments were all a touch too small. The same went for the woman's shoes, which meant she was stuck with the ratty red tennis sneakers, which she pulled on and tied before answering Amelia's latest inquiries.

Sitting again, she folded her hands in her lap as she favored her new creation with an indulgent smile. "I've stayed with my family for a long time without ever once feeling compelled to harm them, but that's only because I'd already been a vampire for a long time before my kids came into the picture. Long enough to learn to control my impulses. You won't have that kind of control for years and years, which means if you care for your family and want them to be safe, you'll have to abandon them."

The tears gathering in Amelia's eyes began to spill down her cheeks. "I can't do that."

Noreen laughed. "Oh yes you can, because if you don't, you'll wind up devouring them. Literally." She laughed again, more exuberantly this time. "As for why I've done this to you, isn't it obvious? This is my revenge against you for fucking my husband. And don't say a word about how you had no choice. I know that already. It doesn't matter. You fucked him. So now I've fucked you. And that's not all. There's something else you should know about new vampires, little Amelia. Would you like me to tell you?"

Amelia was sobbing and needed several moments before she

could pull herself together enough to respond. "Wh-what is it?"

Noreen unclasped her hands and leaned forward in the chair again, smiling brightly as she savored the sweet anticipation of sharing this next part with the emotionally overwhelmed woman. "New vampires are vulnerable in many ways because there's so much they don't know yet. The person who turned them will typically act as a mentor to guide them through these growing pains. But it's more than just that. There is a very real physical and psychological bond. A dependence. When I leave you in a few minutes, you will begin to feel bereft. Abandoned. The mental torture of it will make any human heartbreak you've ever suffered seem insignificant by comparison."

She rose from the chair and approached the bed, snatching her overstuffed handbag off the mattress. "Before you revived, I took the liberty of searching your house and found your purse. The three-hundred dollars in your wallet is gone now. I don't really need it, but I felt like taking it from you, so I did. I'm in need of transportation so I'll be taking your car as well. You will not report it stolen. That is a direct command, Amelia. You'd sooner set yourself on fire than defy your creator. Don't believe me? Feel free to give it a try."

Vindictive laughter resonated in the room as she moved toward the open door.

"Wait."

Noreen stopped at the door and heaved a sigh of exaggerated impatience. As she turned slowly around, a leering grin spread across her face. "I have no more time for you, Amelia. I have to go. My kids are waiting for me."

Amelia got shakily to her feet and wobbled for a moment before stabilizing. "Take me with you."

Noreen cackled, her chest heaving with the force of her mirth. "See? There's that dependence I told you about already kicking in. You're going to be very, very miserable soon, and it's exactly what you deserve."

Amelia rushed toward her, seized her by an arm. "Please. I can't do this alone. I'll do anything. Be your slave. Your lover. Whatever you want."

Noreen backhanded her, sent her spinning across the room until she stumbled and collapsed to the floor. "I don't want you, Amelia, not in any context. I reject you utterly. You are worthless."

Amelia rolled onto her stomach and started crawling across the floor. "Please. Please don't go."

KILL THE HUNTER

Setting a newly created vampire loose in the world without any guidance was a reckless thing to do, perhaps the most reckless thing she'd done since her long ago affair with the nightsider. If Amelia fed within the next twenty-four hours and managed to survive for any significant period of time thereafter, the amount of chaos she might cause could be considerable.

It was a lovely thing to think about.

So much time had passed since she'd last turned someone. Decades. The passage of time had dimmed her memories of how gloriously intoxicating a thing it was, how powerful and god-like it'd made her feel. Despite her best intentions, a part of her was beginning to wonder why she'd left any of this behind.

Amelia was still crawling across the floor.

Noreen kicked her in the face when she came within range.

Then she turned and walked out the door.

EIGHTEEN

ONCE THEY WERE BACK OUT on the interstate, they headed in the opposite direction of Lakemoor and the trail of carnage they'd left behind there. They'd come to no agreement regarding a destination, had barely even discussed it in their hurry to leave the storage facility. As Zach steered them down the highway, the knowledge that the exit to Stillwater Lake was about one-hundred miles in the direction they were going was never far from his mind.

That was just far enough away to feel safely removed from the chaos of the situation they were leaving behind, yet not so far he'd have to spend a dangerously protracted amount of time on the interstate. He felt exposed on the open road. It was still daylight and so many cars, including one police cruiser already, were zipping by them in the passing lane. He was careful to turn his head away as each vehicle passed, trying his best to do it in a way that appeared casual. The worst was when he saw the cop car coming up fast in the rearview mirror. He kept his gaze straight ahead while his hands shook on the steering wheel, but the cop in the cruiser didn't even glance his way as he roared on by.

Chelsea never even noticed the cop. She was in the passenger seat, working to free one of the burner phones from its hard plastic packaging with a knife. It was a big, serrated hunting knife, another of the pilfered items from the storage unit. It looked like it could unzip a man's guts within seconds, but the phone's packaging would not yield easily to the deadly-looking blade.

After a monumental struggle, punctuated with shrieks of rage and frustration, she did finally manage to free the phone from the shredded hard plastic. It came with a cheap charger that had a long, thin black cord. She plugged it into the electrical socket beneath the radio and powered the phone on.

Zach observed all this from the corner of his eye as he drove. "Does it work?"

Chelsea grunted. "Yeah, but I need to activate it."

She retrieved the discarded package from the floor, flipped it over, and started punching in the activation number. A couple minutes passed while she went through a process of punching in numeric responses to the inquiries of the robot voice on the other end.

Then she sighed and glanced at Zach. "All set. It's got some pre-programmed data and talk time, so no need for a credit card."

Zach nodded.

He wasn't sure what use they had for a phone. Not at this juncture anyway. They were avoiding their mother and there was no one else they could safely phone or text. He supposed it would be good to have in the event of some dire emergency, but even then, who would they call? They wouldn't be able to reach out to their mother even if they wanted to, as she'd also disposed of her phone to avoid tracking. It was a scary thing. He didn't think he'd ever felt so untethered from the various safety nets that had kept him protected all his life. When you got right down to it, calling the cops would be the only viable help option if something really bad happened, something they couldn't solve on their own.

He shuddered at the thought.

He was still thinking a lot about the cabin at Stillwater Lake, a property his parents owned under another fake identity. Noreen had told him of the location of a hidden key, a contingency in case anything kept them from reuniting. There was a shed behind the cabin. At the back of the shed, underneath an old barrel, was a little plastic container with the spare key inside. The more he thought about the cabin and that key, the more he became convinced it was where they should go, because what other choice did they truly have?

They weren't hardened criminals wise in the ways of eluding apprehension. No good could come of simply driving and driving without some plan in mind. He imagined them stopping at various convenience stores to gas up the Honda and procure food. They'd just keep running into the same problem that'd plagued them all the way to the storage facility. People would see them. Maybe a lot of people. Someone might recognize them from the news.

There'd be an inherent gamble in being out in any public setting, but they could safely spend a significant period of time stashed away in the cabin at Stillwater Lake. According to their mom, there were no neighbors within visual range, so they'd have a high degree of privacy.

The only problem with hiding out there was a pretty big one.

Mom.

It was safe to assume she'd eventually make her way to the cabin.

Zach kept glancing at Chelsea as he thought about these things. She was playing with the phone, which was some ultra-basic version of a smartphone. He saw a handful of preinstalled apps on the screen.

"Don't log into any of your socials on that thing."

She scowled. "How stupid do you think I am? I'm just looking up local news and looking at Twitter without logging in. I checked some friends' accounts and people are losing their fucking minds."

Zach frowned. "Yeah?"

She nodded. "Also looked at the accounts of some bitches at school who hate me."

Zach's frown deepened. "People hate you? Impossible."

Chelsea laughed. "Show me any halfway popular high school girl who doesn't have at least a few enemies or frenemies and I'll show you a giant sparkly unicorn."

Zach looked confused. "Huh?"

She shrugged. "It doesn't matter. The point is, rumors are flying and the juiciest stuff is coming from those bitches. They're all tweet-storming like Trump on an Adderall bender. One chick keeps saying how she always knew I was bad, that I have a vicious temper and everybody at school is afraid of me. She said, and I quote verbatim, 'It was only a matter of time until she snapped.' People are buying into it too. Fucking cunt."

Zach sighed. "It's just mindless gossip from a shitty person. You can't take it seriously. And there's definitely nothing you can do about it right now. You should probably stop reading that shit."

Chelsea gave her head an adamant shake. "I would, but they're also sharing some real info."

Zach glanced at a road sign coming up on the right.

The exit to Stillwater Lake was now just eighty-seven miles distant. He glanced at his sister. "Yeah? Like what?"

Chelsea's avid gaze was glued to the phone. "Local news links. It's mind-blowing how many there are. It's like a feeding frenzy. You'd think we were Kardashians or something with this much coverage. The cops already found that old lady. 'Robbed at Gunpoint' is one of the headlines. That story has yearbook photos of us next to one of that granny smiling angelically in her Sunday best." She looked up from the screen and stared through the windshield for a moment before glancing at Zach. "This is insane. We're coming off like crazed criminals on an out-of-control spree."

Zach frowned. "Jesus. I guess I can see how it sort of looks that way from the outside, but that's because we're the only ones who know what's really going on. We're nothing like how we're being portrayed. I wish there was some way to get the real story out."

Chelsea sighed heavily, glancing out the windshield again. "No shit, so do I. I don't know what we should do. I'm so confused. So lost. So scared." Tears slid slowly down her face when she next looked at her brother. "Please, Zach, I don't know what to think. Do you have any ideas?"

Zach was silent for a moment as a surprising calmness came over him. During the silence, he marshaled his thoughts, feeling a certainty about what he believed they should do now. He just needed to express it the right way.

He cleared his throat. "The exit to Stillwater Lake is about eighty miles away." He proceeded to explain why he believed they should seek refuge at the cabin, laying out all the reasons that had been bouncing around in his head for the last twenty-some miles. He concluded by saying, "At the very least, it'll give us time to think clearly about everything without feeling pressured. Mom won't get there right away, maybe not for a while yet. Maybe we decide to wait there and take our chances with her. Maybe we use the time to come up with some kind of alternate plan and take off again, I don't know. But I think we need that rest and time to think more than anything."

Chelsea wiped tears from her face and stared out at the road a moment before nodding. "Okay. Yeah. Let's do it."

Zach reached over and squeezed her hand. "We're gonna be okay, Chel. One way or another. Whatever it takes. I promise."

She squeezed his hand back and smiled. "I'll hold you to that."

"I know you will."

Zach gripped the steering wheel firmly in both hands again, keeping his eyes straight ahead as he goosed the gas a bit, taking the Honda up to five miles over the speed limit. An additional few miles per hour wasn't a lot, but if it got them to the cabin even a few minutes faster, it'd be worth it.

NINETEEN

SHE HAD ACTED OUT OF raw emotion, an eruption of molten anger she couldn't have held back even if she'd tried. That was an absolute fact and there was no changing it. What had been done could not be undone. A large part of her still believed it was pointless to feel regretful about things that couldn't be changed, but it happened anyway, second thoughts creeping in within minutes of driving away from the neighborhood she'd lived in for nearly two decades.

To describe what she'd done to the little housewife as reckless was an understatement on a scale almost beyond comprehension. It was a thing she wouldn't have been able to fathom only a few hours ago, when the nice, neatly ordered suburban life she'd created for herself had still been intact. When the savage beast lurking within her had still been tamed and dormant. Draining the one-eyed man had freed the beast and she was shocked by how rapidly and thoroughly it had reclaimed its former hold over her.

When she'd ripped out Amelia's throat, she'd already been in a state of high agitation, filled with rage over her discovery in the tunnel and the things it told her about Jonathan. Amelia's revelations sent her over the edge. In a state like that, a little push was all she'd needed.

She wished she could take it back.

Pointless? Sure.

Nonetheless, she wished like hell she could.

Not because of any misplaced regret over taking a so-called innocent life. What bothered her about her actions went far deeper than that. It represented a loss of control, a surrender to elemental forces that directed her actions in ways superseding her better instincts. The high level of fresh human blood still circulating in her system had a lot to do with it. This was about more than vampiric instincts. It was an addiction, one far stronger than any junkie's craving for heroin.

Her angst over it diminished in intensity as she neared the storage facility, replaced by the anxious anticipation of finally seeing her kids again. She hadn't been able to talk to them in a while. They'd been left to navigate all the potential hazards and pitfalls of a dangerous and evolving situation on their own. She hated that she'd been forced to put them in that position, was plagued by guilt and doubt over it, but at the time it'd been the least awful of a limited range of terrible options. This wasn't just rationalization. She knew it to be true, had known exactly what would be necessary the instant she realized a hunter was in their house, because where there was one hunter, there were always more.

The worst thing about what she'd done to Amelia was the time wasted while waiting around for her resurrection. Vampiric transformation was a curious process. She was aware of no genuine scientific documentation about how it worked, which was unfortunate. Jonathan had shown her long ago and what he'd told her then was still the extent of her knowledge. Transformation started with the introduction of vampiric blood to the human system. As long as this occurred within minutes of death, the consciousness of the person was preserved. Physical healing and reawakening took considerably longer. In Amelia's case, nearly a full hour passed before her eyes opened again, and Noreen had waited all that time just so she could taunt the woman and drink in her misery.

All that selfish foolishness while Zach and Chelsea, mere teenagers, were out there trying to elude the law. By now, they'd either succeeded in making their way to the storage unit or they were in jail.

She flexed her fingers around the steering wheel of the BMW and gritted her teeth as she arrived at the last traffic light she would encounter prior to turning down the road to the storage facility. It'd turned red an infuriating fraction of a second before the driver of the tan Volvo in front of her slammed on their brakes and came to a lurching stop.

Goddammit. Of course.

She itched to go around the Volvo and speed through the intersection before traffic could start moving in the other direction. The only reason she didn't do it was the calmer voice of reason emanating from a more pragmatic corner of her psyche, one that'd been quiet most of the afternoon. That voice told her the light would turn green again in little more than a minute. Whatever awaited her at the storage unit would not change within that tiny window of time. This was not a time for taking unnecessary risks.

Her kids were either there or they were not. She would find out soon.

The light turned bright green.

As soon as she was at last on the street leading to the storage facility, she banged a fist against the steering wheel. This was merely an expenditure of excess stress. There were no more impediments in front of her. She tried to make herself relax, but it was so hard. She knew it wouldn't be fully possible until she was finally able to hold the kids in her arms again.

The facility came into view and she slowed as she arrived at the short drive leading up to the gate. A glance at the rental office as she drove by it revealed nothing to worry about. The only car in the little parking lot belonged to the woman who ran the place. There was no sign of her anywhere outside.

As she pulled up at the gate, she lowered the BMW's driver-side window, leaning out to punch in the security code. Then she sat back and hit the button to raise the window again as the metal gate slowly retracted. The instant it was open wide enough to pass through, she nudged the gas pedal and entered the facility. As she drove forward, she glanced at her rearview mirror, checking for signs of being observed. There was no indication of it.

In less than another minute, she pulled up in front of unit 612.

No other cars were parked anywhere in the vicinity. She saw nothing but closed steel doors and the wide, open space between rows of units. This alone portended nothing ominous. She'd told the kids to ditch the stolen car somewhere nearby and walk the remaining distance to the facility. The absence of a vehicle was an indication they'd followed her instructions. They might yet be on the other side of the closed door to unit 612.

Then she saw the combination lock hanging from the door hasp, the u-shaped shackle clicked firmly into place. Her heart sank at the sight of it, another strong surge of anxiety rising within her. The one thing this told her with absolute certainty was that her kids were not currently inside the unit. The anticipated reunion was no longer as imminent as she'd hoped.

A part of her was inclined to fear the worst, that the kids had been apprehended or perhaps even killed by trigger-happy police. She'd taken the time to watch some news at Amelia's house while awaiting her resurrection and was keenly aware of how blown out of proportion the situation had become. Her kids weren't dangerous spree killers, but the cops didn't know that.

She tried calming her nerves by telling herself their absence here didn't necessarily mean anything other than that they'd been delayed. Unknown circumstances might have arisen, forcing them to hide out somewhere else for a while. Unfortunately, she possessed no magical mental link to the kids, and couldn't know anything with any degree of certainty. There was an inherent sense of powerlessness in this realization, a feeling she didn't care for one bit.

Part of her wanted to go out looking for them, but her more logical side vetoed the idea as obviously nonsensical. She was likelier to find the proverbial needle in a haystack than locate her kids with a lot of random driving around. No, the only sensible thing to do was wait for them here and hope they eventually showed up.

She got out of the BMW and threw the door shut, the agitation she was feeling causing her to put a bit more force into it than necessary. The sound of the door slamming was like the crack of a gunshot echoing in the space between unit rows.

A few quick spins of the combination lock's dial popped it open. She dropped the lock in her handbag, grabbed the door's handle, and heaved it upward. With the door open, an instinctive first step forward happened, but she came to a dead stop almost immediately, a lump forming in her throat when she saw the big empty space formerly occupied by the Honda Accord.

The car had been there the last time she'd visited the unit. In the time since then, someone had opened the unit and taken the car. There were just two possibilities she could think of, and she wasn't sure which of them was the more disturbing one. Either Jonathan had returned to town at some recent point without informing her and taken the Accord, or her kids had shown up here earlier this afternoon and driven away with it, counter to her instructions.

She could imagine Jonathan doing something that sneaky and

underhanded. It'd be right in line with everything he'd done over the last year, the way he'd given priority to his own selfish needs over the needs of his family. There was a problem with that, though. Selfish he was, yes. Underhanded too. But Noreen couldn't see him returning just to retrieve a twenty-year-old Honda Accord from a dingy storage unit when he had the cash to buy a much better, brand-new car outright wherever he happened to be now.

So logic told her a sadder story.

Her kids had been here. Had arrived well ahead of her, in fact. Out of natural curiosity, they explored and examined the contents of the unit, finding much to disturb them. Zach and Chelsea were human kids who knew nothing of the vampiric nature of their parents. Knew nothing of the secret lives they'd lived. They'd seen the vast array of weaponry and had looked inside the refrigerator. Maybe they'd opened the Accord's trunk and found the bags stuffed full of millions in cash, a revelation that would have instantly destroyed the long-maintained illusion of their parents as hard-working ordinary suburbanites who sometimes struggled to get by. All of it would have been upsetting on numerous levels, not the least of which was the lies upon lies it all represented, but the worst discovery of all might have been what was lying inside the open casket at the rear of the unit.

Noreen ran to the casket and leaned over it to peer inside, groaning loudly in relief at what she saw. The old nightsider bastard had not yet started to regenerate, at least not in any visible way. Keeping him sealed inside the casket was crucial. She thumbed a button to unlock the hinges holding the lid up and slammed it down, shuddering at the close call. If she'd arrived closer to twilight, she might not have been able to stop him from coming back.

She had enough to deal with without having to battle a pissed off old nightsider hungry for revenge. The casket and its occupant should have been fed through a crematory oven years ago, but Jonathan had objected, insisting there was value in holding onto the evil bastard's remains. This might even have been true, assuming they were willing to engage with other parties every bit as dangerous. Well, Jonathan wasn't part of the equation anymore, and Noreen wanted no part of that madness. The casket was getting incinerated as soon as she could arrange it.

She moved away from the coffin and examined the wall of weaponry, discerning right away that some things had been removed. Guns and some of the edged weapons. A fair amount of ammunition, judging from the somewhat depleted contents of the open crates on the floor. Her kids had departed this place, but not before gearing up for war. It made her nervous as hell, but it was better than thinking about them being out there with only minimal means of defending themselves.

Where would they have gone after leaving the facility?

Maybe to the cabin at Stillwater Lake, per the original plan, or they might be heading somewhere else altogether out of a newfound fear of their mother. Somewhere she wouldn't know about. They'd seen many scary things. The woman they'd thought she was didn't really exist. They would feel angry and betrayed. Unsure they could trust anything they'd ever been told.

These things were beyond her control.

All she could do was go to Stillwater Lake and hope.

She turned away from the wall of weapons and looked out toward the unit's open door, her body freezing with tension again at what she saw standing just inside the entrance. The man was huge, twice the size of the one-eyed intruder at her house, and that man had been an imposing physical presence in his own right. This man was around six and a half feet tall with the build of a champion weightlifter. Lots of black body armor covered the more vulnerable parts of his physical form. He had a head like a slab of granite, with a thick beard and long brown hair. Gripped in his massive right hand was a short sword with a deadly-looking blade.

He smiled as their gazes met.

A sense of resignation settled within Noreen as she shifted to a fighting stance. "Let me guess. You're the Annihilator."

His smile broadened, becoming the grin of a man about to do the thing he enjoyed most in the world, the thing he'd been born to do.

Annihilate.

He nodded and uttered a single syllable. "Yes."

They ran at each other.

TWENTY

THE JOURNEY TO STILLWATER LAKE ran into a complication when Chelsea was assailed by a wave of intense nausea that had her moaning and squirming in her seat. They were still forty miles from the Stillwater Lake exit by then, making it a situation where she would not be able to fight through it and hold on until they got there.

Her face turned red and sweat rose on her brow, beads of it trickling down the sides of her face from her temples. The squirming gave way to a rocking motion as she unbuckled her seatbelt and lowered the window on her side.

"I'm gonna be sick," she told her brother, teeth chattering as she turned away from him and stuck her head out the open window. "Please stop the car."

Zach frowned.

He checked the rearview and side mirrors for cop cruisers and saw only civilian vehicles. That was good. Stopping at the side of the interstate was not good. A cop cruiser or highway patrol car was bound to come along before long. Absent signs of a serious emergency, they might pass on by without stopping. Or they might not. He'd only been driving about a year and a half and still couldn't reliably predict how cops on the highway would operate in every situation. Even with no obvious indication of an emergency, they might stop and check on a pulled over motorist on a mere whim, or out of boredom.

Chelsea moaned again. "Please, Zach. I'm gonna fucking puke."

Despite his misgivings, he understood he had no real choice here. He couldn't let her suffer, and the next exit wasn't yet in sight. Stopping at a convenience store or fast-food joint off the highway wouldn't be a great option either. They were sixty miles down the highway from their hometown—and even farther from Lakemoor—but that probably wasn't far enough to take them beyond the viewing area of their local television stations. Not that it mattered considering how widely their pictures had circulated on social media. The risk of being recognized in any public place was climbing with every passing second.

He put on his blinker to stay within the requirements of the law as he began to slow down and ease the Accord over to the shoulder. A guy in one of those giant oversized pickup trucks favored by douchebags everywhere honked, making him flinch. Not for the first time that day, his hands tightened around the steering wheel as he fought the impulse to make an obscene gesture.

Once he was fully off the pavement and on the shoulder of the road, the truck roared by, the driver leaning on the horn to produce a long, obnoxious blast of jarring sound. As soon as they'd come to a full stop, Chelsea threw open the passenger side door and vaulted out of the car.

Zach watched her stagger toward the guardrail, stopping a few feet short of it as she bent over at the waist and started making loud hacking noises. The sound was awful and grating, like the dry running of a kitchen garbage disposal. She kept at it for at least a minute without disgorging anything and for a moment he allowed himself the hope this might be the end of it.

The sickness had come over her so quickly, without any warning at all, making him wonder if it might be a delayed physical reaction to all the stress and excitement of the day. She'd been through a lot, having shot and killed at least one person and probably a second, though according to her account, she hadn't been able to see the driver of the GTO and thus couldn't know his fate. He had been wounded at the very least. Factor in the gunpoint theft of a saintly old lady's car and the revelations of the storage unit, and, well . . . it was a lot. In truth, he didn't feel that great himself. He'd just been hoping to put off having a total breakdown until reaching the cabin.

The hacking sounds from Chelsea soon gave way to queasiersounding noises that made Zach think of a cat trying to cough out a hairball, only amplified by a factor of about ten. This was followed by a loud belch like something he'd expect to hear from a frat boy jock at a kegger, not from his little sister. As he watched, she bent over further still and screamed in distress for a moment before ejecting a long stream of yellow-tinged vomit that splashed at her feet and got her shoes wet.

"Are you all right out there?"

She moaned again and tried to say something that emerged as an unintelligible jumble, but he understood well enough. She was telling him he'd asked a stupid question and he had to admit she had a point. The sounds emerging from her throat were not those of a person who was "all right." His level of concern increased sharply as she spewed more vomit. He'd hoped this would be a quick-passing thing, but maybe she was sicker than he'd imagined. Maybe it had nothing to do with stress.

Zach checked his mirrors again.

Still no cops, but some of the cars passing by on the highway slowed as they drove by, the drivers taking long looks. Once again, he tried to keep his head turned away, but that trick could only work for so long before someone decided he was acting suspiciously and called the police.

After checking yet again to make sure he wouldn't get plowed over by an oncoming vehicle, Zach opened the door on his side and eased it to a semi-shut position before hurrying around to the other side and approaching his sister. He put a tentative hand to the middle of her back and said, "I don't mean to sound insensitive, but we're really vulnerable out here like this."

"Do you think I don't know that?" she snapped back. "I'm not doing this on purpose."

He nodded. "I know. I'm sorry. But the second you feel like you're even mildly stabilized, we need to be back in the car and moving on down the fucking road."

Chelsea let out a big groan and abruptly stood up straight, flipping her long hair away from her face. The long locks had wet flecks of yellow embedded in them. Her face twisted in a mixture of pain and disgust as she turned away from Zach and staggered toward the car.

Zach turned and watched her. "You sure you're ready?"

"*Yes!*"

The one word was nearly a scream. It told him she wasn't sure about anything but lacked the energy to discuss the matter while standing around on the side of a busy road. She opened the passenger side door after pulling at the handle a few times to get a firm enough grip on it. Then she dropped into the passenger seat like a sack of dead weight and pulled the door shut again.

After a moment, she turned her head and looked at Zach through bleary eyes. "Are you coming or not?"

Zach nodded. "Yeah."

He waited for the lane to clear again and hurried around to the driver-side door and yanked it open, sliding in behind the wheel. He glanced at his sister as he started the engine. She was sitting in a slumped position with her seatbelt off and her head lolling to one side, foam at the corners of her mouth and spittle all over her chin.

Noticing his scrutiny, she sat up a little straighter. "Go, Zach."

He nodded but had to wait for an 18-wheeler and two trailing compact cars to pass by before making his move. After easing the Accord back onto solid blacktop, he pushed the gas pedal almost to the floor and held it there until he was back up to speed with highway traffic. He eased off as soon as the speedometer hit 75 MPH, then checked his mirrors yet again, feeling some of the tension that had been building inside him slip away upon seeing no flashing blue lights closing in.

They drove without speaking for several minutes. During that time, Chelsea uttered the occasional soft moan and shifted slightly in her seat. She held her hand lightly against her stomach, barely touching it while appearing to derive some comfort from the slight pressure.

Zach cleared his throat. "So . . . that was kind of out of nowhere. Did you eat anything today that might have caused that?"

She gave her head a weak shake. "All I've had today was some toast for breakfast. If anything, the lack of food in my stomach made that worse. I couldn't get anything up, but I was nauseous as hell and my fucking stomach felt like it was trying to turn itself inside out."

Zach nodded, thinking of the horrible dry, hacking sounds she'd made after getting out of the car. "Huh. Strange."

She sat up straighter still and wiped moisture from her mouth with the back of a hand. Her head turned slowly toward him and she studied him with an inscrutable expression before saying, "If I tell you something, do you promise not to overreact?"

He frowned, glancing at her. "Um . . . I guess? Whatever it is, you should probably tell me anyway. Holding back possibly important info won't help anything."

She grunted. "Okay. I first felt something when I leaned over that coffin. You know how sometimes when you're out in public and out of nowhere you feel a little tickle at the back of your throat, the kind you get right at the start of a cold or a bad case of the flu? Nine times out of ten, it's because you got too close to some super sick person without knowing it, some selfish fucker who should be home in bed instead of out in public infecting other people."

Zach felt a stirring of uneasiness.

He knew what she meant, had experienced that very thing more than once, but he didn't see how it could possibly apply here. She'd leaned over the corpse in the coffin, but she hadn't touched it, nor had she gotten any closer to it than he had. Yes, he was stressed to the max and hovering on the edge of a breakdown, but he felt no symptoms of physical sickness. Not the faintest stirring. He was no medical expert by any means, but he didn't think you could catch the flu from a rotting corpse, especially one well past the grossest stages of bloat and decomposition. Maybe you could pick up some other nasty form of bacteria by shoving your hand or face into its innards, some insane thing like that, but otherwise he couldn't see it.

Yet that feeling of uneasiness remained, largely because he had the lingering sense there was something unusual about the corpse in the coffin, something beyond the mere fact of its inexplicable presence in the storage unit. Which was why instead of giving voice to all this doubt, he merely nodded and prompted her to go on by saying, "Yeah. And?"

She sighed, a sound heavily invested with frustration and more than a little fear. "I know it sounds crazy, but I really feel like whatever this is started when I leaned over that dead fucker. Like I breathed in something bad." She surprised him with a sudden teary sniffle. "Zach, I'm scared. You're thinking none of this makes any sense. I can see it in your face. But I'm telling you, it started there, and whatever it is, it's fucked up and strange. We saw enough at that place to know Mom and Dad are fucked up and strange, like not in any kind of normal world way. What if it's something a regular doctor can't help me with?"

Zach drove on in thoughtful silence for over a minute before responding. "It doesn't matter how it sounds. You're right, normal went out the window a while ago. I believe you."

She sniffled again. "Thank you."

Zach smiled in what he hoped was a reassuring way. "Of course. It's like I already told you. Whatever it takes, we're getting through this."

She nodded, but still looked troubled. "But what do we do now?"

Zach shrugged. "I still don't see any magic solution. We'll head up to the cabin as planned, but now I'm thinking we definitely wait there until Mom shows up. *Hopefully* shows up. If whatever you're feeling is somehow connected to that thing in the coffin, she might be the only person with any idea what the problem is and how to fix it."

The look on Chelsea's face betrayed doubt and anxiety. "Okay. I'm still scared of her and don't know if I can ever really trust her again, but you're right. It's our only real chance to figure any of this out."

The next half hour passed mostly in silence, brother and sister spending that time lost in their own thoughts as the miles rolled away. When they got to within ten miles of the exit to Stillwater Lake, Zach nudged the Accord's speed close to 80 MPH, the fastest he'd dared to go the entire time they were on the interstate. At one point, a police cruiser did finally come along in the passing lane, its appearance triggering the usual jolt of tension, but it moved swiftly along at a speed matching the flow of traffic. The cop behind the wheel never even looked Zach's way.

A few minutes after that, Zach put on his blinker and took the exit to Stillwater Lake.

TWENTY-ONE

NOREEN WENT STRAIGHT AT THE man called the Annihilator, moving with explosive vampiric speed. The hunter started swinging his sword in the same instant as he rushed toward her. It was a move she recognized from long ago encounters with other hunters, a calculated compensation for her superior speed, but instead of chopping through her neck, it sliced only through empty air.

She'd gone into a slide at the last possible instant, grabbing him by the ankles and jerking his feet out from under him. The man's sword flew from his hand and went clattering across the unit's concrete floor as he pitched forward, the momentum of his falling body such that he didn't have time to brace himself. His bearded chin hit the concrete with a loud crack, eliciting a sound from the hunter that was more a snarl of rage than a cry of pain.

He surged to his feet almost as quickly as Noreen, but he wasn't able to turn around in time to deflect the running leap she took at him. Her right foot slammed into his lower back, causing him to stagger forward a few steps before he went sprawling on the floor again. She pressed her advantage, leaping upon him and straddling his back as she grabbed him by the neck and reached for the front of his throat. A quick end to this battle by severing his jugular vein was what she had in mind, but he swiftly raised himself up from the floor. He did this with surprising ease, considering she remained locked around his midsection, her fingers still probing for vulnerable flesh.

She saw him reaching for a knife in a sheath strapped to his thigh and distracted him by taking a bite out of his right ear, sweet, fresh blood spurting into her mouth as she swallowed his earlobe. He unleashed a howl of rage and pain and started punching at her with one of his massive fists, landing several direct hits. She was largely impervious to the pummeling at first, being still amped up from all the blood she'd consumed, but this was a man of unusual strength. After absorbing several hard blows to little discernible effect, the next few broke through the vampiric pain barrier, rendering her slightly woozy.

When he felt her grip on him loosening, he grabbed hold of her arms and executed a maneuver that flipped her over his head. She went flying toward the unit's open door, skidding forward several feet after hitting the concrete. By the time she managed to roll over, the giant hunter was standing right over her. Instead of retrieving his sword, he'd plucked the large double-bladed axe from the wall of edged weapons. He sneered in triumph as he planted a heavy, booted foot on her stomach and began to raise the axe.

His mistake this time was in taking that extra moment to savor apparent victory over his quarry. The man was three times her size at least, maybe more, with an upper body mass like that of a bull. Against any human mortal on the planet, he would prevail in virtually any physical contest. But Noreen wasn't human and the slight pause was all the time she needed to marshal her superior strength. She seized the ankle of the foot pressed to her stomach in both hands and gave it a savage twist.

The hunter howled again, dropping the double-bladed axe and falling as she relinquished her grip on him. He hit the ground with a heavy thud, but once again began to rise almost immediately, this time with a groan of pain.

Noreen and the hunter fully regained their feet at the same time, eying each other warily from a distance of about six feet just inside the unit's open door. They moved in a slow circle, maintaining the distance as the man made low, throaty sounds like the growling of a hungry animal. After three careful revolutions, his hand went to the knife strapped to his thigh, removed it, and sent it flying toward Noreen in one impressively smooth and quick motion. She saw the point of the heavy blade coming straight at the center of her face and jerked her head to the side just in time to avoid it, smiling when she heard it smack against the refrigerator directly behind her. A direct hit wouldn't have killed her, but it might well have given him an opportunity to get in close enough to inflict more lethal damage.

A steady trickle of blood was still dripping from the man's injured ear. "Your blood is the best I've tasted today. Earthier. Wilder. You'd make an incredible vampire."

The hunter chuckled as they continued circling. "I'd rather die than become an abomination like you. While tracking you, I stumbled across the one you turned today. Such a pitiful creature. She tried to attack me, feed from me, but I took her head off with my sword and set her remains on fire in the yard behind her house. It was glorious, the way it always is when—"

They'd moved deeper into the unit as they circled and talked, with Noreen studying the wall of weapons as surreptitiously as possible. With each revolution, she was within optimal range of the wall for a couple seconds at a time. On the eighth or ninth revolution, while the assassin was still immersed in his gloating speech and she was again close to the wall, Noreen flexed her legs and leapt up from the floor.

The bottoms of her sneakers touched the edge of the long table beneath the array of weapons just long enough for her to snag the handle of the heavy mace from its peg and push off again. She did a complete backflip away from the table, soaring over the hunter's head as she began to swing the mace. He tried taking another swipe at her with yet another long blade produced from somewhere on his person, but she'd put him off-balance and he was too slow anyway. The heavy iron ball at the end of the chain was already arcing toward the side of his head as she landed on her feet behind him.

An electric thrill of exhilaration and triumph crackled through her system as several long iron spikes thudded into his head at the temple, fully penetrating his skull and entering his brain. He remained on his feet but became clumsier, making grunting sounds as he tried to turn in a circle again, staggering with each leaden step. The blade he'd pulled moments ago slipped from his fingers. Noreen held onto the handle of the mace and stayed with him as he moved, giving the handle a tug every few seconds that made him moan and attempt to utter words that emerged as gibberish. The third time she did this he produced a pitiful squeal that made him sound like a scared puppy.

He dropped to his knees.

Still gripping the handle, Noreen put her face close to the side of his head that didn't have a big iron ball stuck in it. She lapped at the blood still trickling from his ear and laughed softly. "It's funny, isn't it?"

He swayed on his knees, on the verge of toppling over.

Noreen laughed again. "They called you the Annihilator, but now I've annihilated you, so tell me asshole, which one of us is really more deserving of that name?"

The defeated hunter's only answer was another moan.

Noreen's hands tightened on the handle in preparation of ripping the spikes from the man's head. Before she could do it, a shriek emanated from outside the unit. She looked up and saw a slender middle-aged woman with brown hair standing near the stolen BMW. The woman had her hands up in front of her face and was shaking so hard she looked on the verge of melting. It took Noreen a moment to recognize her as the woman who ran the rental office.

The woman's mouth moved as she tried and failed to speak.

Noreen sighed. "I'd ask you why you're poking your nose into my business, but there's really no point. You've seen too much."

She ripped the spikes from the hunter's head with a savage yank on the mace's handle. Blood jetted from the holes in his head as he began to topple sideways. The woman clapped splayed fingers to her face again and screamed.

Then she turned and ran.

Noreen dropped the mace and chased after her, catching up to her within seconds. She grabbed her around the waist and clamped a hand over her mouth, stifling another scream. The woman struggled mightily, but Noreen held her still with ease. After looking around and seeing no one else in the space between unit rows, she carried the woman into the open unit and dumped her on the floor.

She pulled the roller door down and moved into the middle of the unit, standing there with her hands on her hips as she looked back and forth between her human captives. The hunter was brain-damaged and on his way out, still losing a lot of blood, but she thought he might yet have a few minutes of consciousness remaining. Whether he was actually still perceiving anything in any meaningful way was questionable. She hoped so. Just for a tiny bit longer.

She grinned in a leering way. "I'm quite angry with both of you for meddling in my business. I should go looking for my kids, but I think you need to pay a heavy price for your interference. So I'm going to spend a little extra time playing with you both."

The woman from the rental office sat up and scooted backward until her back met the refrigerator. "Please . . . don't hurt me. I won't . . ." She looked over at the dying man, grimacing at the grisly sight of his wounds. "I won't tell anybody about any of this."

Noreen nodded. "Yes. I know."

She moved so fast the woman only had time to gasp before Noreen's fangs penetrated the soft flesh of her throat.

TWENTY-TWO

THE CABIN WAS LOCATED SEVERAL winding miles off the interstate, way up in the hills surrounding Stillwater Lake. A narrow private drive a shade over half a mile in length led up to the property, the curving ribbon of faded and pitted asphalt bracketed by towering stands of lush old trees. About halfway up the drive, Zach had to stop and wait for a deer to take its sweet time moving out of the way. He didn't mind because the sight of it perked Chelsea up slightly for just a moment, making her smile and mumble a word that sounded like "pretty."

Once the deer had moved out of the way, he continued the rest of the way up at a slower speed, wary of colliding with another creature of the forest, but they encountered no further obstructions. That was a relief. He needed a break from the non-stop stress of their hours-long ordeal as much as Chelsea. Running into or over some innocent animal right before finally arriving at a place of shelter and safety would have been too much to take.

His mouth dropped open as he steered the Accord around a bend in the narrow drive and the cabin came into view. It was not as rustic or run-down as he'd imagined. On the way up here from the interstate, his mind had flashed back to the broken-down old shack in Lakemoor. He'd pictured something a bit like that, albeit perhaps slightly better maintained. What he saw instead was a nice-looking A-frame log house. It was of a modest size, but had two floors and a long, railed porch in front with a short set of steps at either end. There was a wide parking area in front with room enough for several large vehicles, but the Accord was the only one present. Another narrow length of gray asphalt diverged from the paved area and appeared to go around to the back of the house.

Zach pointed in that direction. "We should probably go that way. Park the car out of sight."

Chelsea shrugged. "Whatever you think."

There was resignation in her voice, an implied willingness to cede all decision-making to him for the time being, but she didn't sound as strained as before, the hoarseness fading. The improvement was marginal but it was better than no improvement at all. He hated to admit it, even just to himself, but her talk of being somehow infected by the rotting corpse from the storage unit had gotten to him. He'd started thinking maybe it was true, even though it defied all logic. If her condition had worsened, he'd be out of his mind with worry by now.

He gave the Accord's steering wheel a little leftward tug, guiding it toward the narrow side drive. As he pulled around back, he spied the storage shed his mother had told him about. A smirk came to his face. The shed by itself was nearly as large as the broken-down shack in Lakemoor. In retrospect, it'd been silly to imagine his parents owning a property anywhere close to that downtrodden, given what he now knew about their vast, hidden wealth.

Another dense expanse of tall trees stood directly behind the shed, but a rock-covered trail to the right led down to a long pier and the placid-looking lake. This time of day was right on the cusp of that divide between late afternoon and early evening, the sun still just high enough in the sky to maintain full daylight a short while longer. Its rays glinted on the softly rippling, blue-green water. An unexpected serenity came over Zach at the sight of the natural beauty. He knew the feeling was illusory and fleeting, that they were still potentially in a lot of trouble, but it sure felt nice in that moment.

He parked the car near the back porch and cut the engine off. "I guess I'll go look for that key."

Her gaze was focused on the trail and the pier beyond as she said, "It's so nice here. Do you think we'll be able to stay a while?"

Zach shrugged. "I don't know. I guess we'll have to see what happens."

He knew it was a lame response even as he uttered the words, but he didn't want to commit to any kind of definitive statement on the matter. Staying as positive as possible was one thing. He wanted to keep her morale up. His own, too. But he didn't have one clue what their immediate future held and knew it'd be best not to pretend otherwise.

"Get out of the car and stretch your legs. Breathe some fresh air. I'll be right back."

She nodded. "Okay."

He opened the driver-side door, got out, and took a deep breath of his own, inhaling the earthy scents of the forest and the lake. It felt cleansing, another sensation he knew was at least partially illusory, a product of suggestion, but there was something real about the feeling as well. He looked over the roof of the car and saw Chelsea yawn as she stretched her arms and looked up at the sky. His worries aside, he hoped they'd get to stay here a while. It might do them both a lot of good.

Before going to the back of the shed, he walked up to its front door and rattled the doorknob. Locked, as he'd expected. He circled around to the back and saw two old wooden barrels where their mother said they'd be, right against the shed beneath a set of small, heavily smudged double windows. One of the barrels was in much worse shape than the other. It had several holes in it and was split open at the seams, the rusted metal bands loose at the top and bottom. The other barrel was also clearly many decades old but intact.

That was the one he wanted.

The barrel's rust-encrusted metal lid was screwed down tight, rendered impossible to open without a crowbar. He wasn't here to see what was inside it anyway. Testing the barrel's weight by pushing at its top, he found that it wasn't exactly lightweight, but it felt moveable. There was something inside it, but at least it didn't feel like it was packed with cement, as he'd feared. He grabbed hold of it and began pulling it away from the wall in a semi-circular motion, moving it about a foot away from the shed with each turn. This required a fair amount of exertion, causing sweat to rise on his brow.

Breathing hard, he looked down at the barren ground formerly covered by the barrel's bottom. Nestled there in the soft earth with squirming earthworms and assorted other bugs was the plastic keyholder. He snatched it up and snapped it open, dumping the key into his palm. Having the key in his hand was a good feeling, one that came with a minor sense of accomplishment. At this point he was grateful for anything that worked out right. Or maybe it wasn't such a small thing. Without it, they would've been faced with the dilemma of whether to break into the cabin. The place probably didn't have an alarm system, at least not an activated one, otherwise Noreen Murphy would've mentioned it.

He spent a moment considering whether he should return the barrel to its previous spot but dismissed the idea quickly. It'd require another expenditure of energy and what did it really matter now anyway if he left the old barrel a few feet from where he'd found it? He was on the verge of returning to the parking area behind the cabin when a sudden impulse caused him to approach the double windows for a peek inside the shed.

The small windows were positioned at about the level of his chest, but the heavily smudged glass appeared not to have been cleaned in many years. Also, it was dark inside the structure, and the back of the shed was currently facing away from the sun. The dense stand of tall trees looming behind Zach also impeded visibility to some degree. He nonetheless got close to the glass, framing his face with his hands in an effort to discern anything obscured by hazy shadows. At first he wasn't able to make out much at all, but then what daylight remained allowed him to faintly perceive a familiar shape.

Atop what looked like an old worktable was a coffin.

In fact, there were two of them.

The shock of sudden recognition caused Zach to reel backward several steps. His heart was beating so fast he felt dizzy, unable to control the panicked reaction. He stood there frozen for several additional moments, the terror of this new discovery too much to process. The spell wasn't broken until he heard his sister calling for him from the other side of the shed.

He swallowed a lump in his throat. "Be right there."

He forced his gaze away from the smudged windows, trying not to overthink what he'd glimpsed as he circled back around to the parking area. He couldn't write off what he'd seen as a trick of the fading light. There were coffins in the shed. This was indisputable. Their presence was troubling, but he had to put it in perspective. After their experience at the storage unit, this new discovery could not fairly be called a complete surprise. As long as they left these coffins undisturbed, there shouldn't be a problem. The solution was simple.

They'd stay away from the shed, and they sure as hell wouldn't go inside it.

Chelsea was standing with her arms crossed near the cabin's back porch as he returned, an inquisitive look on her face. "What took so long?"

Zach shrugged. "The barrel was fucking heavy."

"But you got the key?"

He raised his hand, showing it to her. "Yep."

Her pale features registered relief. "Thank God."

Zach decided he wouldn't tell her about what he'd seen, at least for now. She was paranoid enough about her exposure to the corpse at the storage unit. Hearing about these other coffins would only unnecessarily heighten her sense of worry. The coffins couldn't open themselves, after all. His basic line of reasoning was that what she didn't know couldn't hurt her.

He sincerely hoped that was true.

Up on the porch, he slid the key into the lock, mouthing a silent prayer his assumptions about the lack of an alarm were on the money. Exhaling once the key was inside the lock, he began to turn the doorknob, pushing at the door when he heard the click signaling the lock's disengagement.

The door moved inward, away from the frame.

No alarm sounded.

He heaved an audible sigh of relief.

Chelsea grunted. "Why do you sound like a bomb technician in a movie who just cut the right wire seconds before detonation?"

Zach laughed, glancing back at her. "Because I was worried about an alarm. Don't know what the fuck we would've done if there'd been one."

Chelsea smirked. "We would've gotten the fuck out of here."

Zach nodded.

After pushing the door fully open, he walked into a kitchen that was smaller than the one back home—their *former* home—but was outfitted with shiny new stainless-steel appliances and a sturdy oak dining table over by a large window. Lacy curtains were pulled shut over the glass. A look around revealed that all the windows were similarly covered. The only illumination was courtesy of the sunlight streaming in through the open door.

Zach looked to his left and saw switches on the wall by the door. He flipped the switches up and bright light flooded the room. The power not being on had been another of his many background worries. A refrigerator in a corner of the kitchen was humming away smoothly.

Chelsea brushed by him, going to the fridge and opening the door. "Of course," she said, after a longish pause, during which her gaze was fixed on the appliance's interior. Then she looked at her brother. "More fucking blood. And beer."

Zach frowned.

He approached the fridge and looked inside, seeing numerous fat blood pouches, though not nearly as many as they'd found at the storage unit. A couple dozen maybe, all piled up on the top shelf. On the middle shelf were three six-packs of craft beer, all selections from Three Floyds Brewing, including Zombie Dust Pale Ale.

Jonathan Murphy's favorite.

Brother and sister looked at each other, eyes widening in alarm.

They'd each missed their father intensely at various times during his long, unexplained absence. As time had gone on, the ache was often displaced by resentment and even something resembling hatred. He'd put them through hell for no reason they could understand. On top of all that, it seemed apparent he was the root cause for all the horrible things they'd gone through today. Yes, their mother wasn't quite the innocent they'd always imagined, but at least she'd not abandoned them. For all these reasons and more, the prospect of a possible reunion with their father brought no sense of joy or relief.

Quite the opposite.

Zach cleared his throat. "He's not here. There's no other cars. The beer's probably been here a while."

Chelsea nodded. "Uh-huh. Or he's just gone out somewhere and is coming back soon."

Shit.

It was an entirely plausible point.

"Fuck it."

Zach reached into the fridge and took one of the beers out, then started looking around for a bottle opener.

Chelsea frowned.

Then she shrugged and followed suit.

Zach raised an eyebrow at the sight of the bottle in her hand. "You're not old enough."

She rolled her eyes. "Neither are you in the eyes of the law.

Besides, we're outlaws now. Remember?"

Zach laughed as he started pulling open drawers. "Point taken. I'm just surprised you feel up to having a beer after being sick."

She shrugged. "It's weird. I feel almost completely better. I don't know how, but I do. Anyway, I've never had a beer or any other kind of alcohol drink. It'd be nice to have the experience before I die."

Zach found what he was looking for and pried the cap off his own bottle before passing the opener to Chelsea. "That's not happening any time soon, Chel."

She popped open her bottle of Zombie Dust, allowing the cap to fall to the floor at her feet. "You don't know that. We have no idea what's gonna happen. Dad might show up. The cops might track us here. I don't know how, but they might. Those scary people looking for Dad might show up, and if that happens, we might be fucked."

He heard the fear in her voice and nodded, knowing there wasn't much he could say to refute her words.

After finishing his beer, Zach went back outside and started bringing in all the stuff they'd pilfered from the storage unit.

Starting with the guns.

TWENTY-THREE

THE STORY WAS STILL BEING covered on all the local stations, but it'd been a while since any new information had come to light. Reporters were still doing live segments from various locations, including from the convenience store in Lakemoor and outside the Murphy family home, where multiple news trucks were lined up on the street.

A lot of background activity was evident in the wide-angle shots from the convenience store segments. Multiple police cruisers with blue lights flashing were visible, as was an ambulance with its back doors standing open. Officers were shown talking to witnesses, many of whom had already provided soundbites to the news crews. The soundbites were being replayed into oblivion, especially one involving an especially hysterical woman juggling multiple young children, including a surly-looking toddler in a Kid Rock T-shirt.

More grimly interesting to Elliot Valentine was the oft-repeated clip of someone in a body bag being loaded into the ambulance. It was a stark and disturbing reminder how high stakes the situation had become, and of how potentially perilous his own position was. The explosion of chaotic, widespread violence was not at all what he'd expected to happen today.

That he knew the people involved was upsetting enough, but what made it almost unbearably distressing was knowing he'd set these bloody events in motion. He'd expected a quick and clean operation with no violence and no lasting consequences for anyone other than, ultimately, Jonathan Murphy. Instead, the outcome was a spiraling clusterfuck, a whirlwind of chaos he feared would only continue to become more and more destructive.

The knock at his front door came while he was pacing the house, just as he'd returned to the living room to scoop up the remote and start flipping through the local stations again. He stood stock-still at first, such was his surprise at hearing the knock. Uninvited callers were rare thanks to the large and aggressively worded sign warning away solicitors mounted inside his screen door. He had a few neighbors who might come looking for him to chat or inquire about this or that at random times, but they were not usually around this time of day.

Enough time passed after the knock that he began to think perhaps he'd imagined it. Or perhaps his ears had played a trick on him, picking up a similar sound from somewhere outside. Like, for instance, someone from up the street pounding a nail into a piece of lumber. Then the knocking sound came again, louder and more aggressive than the first time, leaving no room for mistake. Someone was at his door and was trying hard to get his attention.

He put the remote down and walked out of the living room and into the foyer. There were narrow vertical windows covered by gauzy curtains to either side of the door, but he didn't want the person on the porch to see him glancing out through them. Moving as quietly as he could, he went to the door and put an eye to the peephole.

A woman was standing on the porch. She was wearing dark sunglasses and had a scarf on her head, one that hid her hair entirely. The scarf threw him off because he couldn't remember ever seeing her with her hair fully covered, but soon enough he recognized her anyway. She'd been looking off to one side when he first put his eye to the peephole, but now she was staring straight at the door. The exquisite planes of her achingly pretty face had the usual effect, taking his breath away while making him feel hopelessly inadequate on every level. She was a rare, ethereal goddess, and he was nothing. This was how he'd always felt, but it didn't matter. He wanted her anyway, desired her love more than anything else on earth.

He unlocked and opened the door.

"Noreen, what are you—"

She pushed past him into the foyer, urging him to quickly close the door. He did so, but not before noticing the black BMW convertible parked on the street at the edge of his yard. No one was inside it and it wasn't a car he recognized. He could only assume Noreen had driven it here, but where had she gotten it? The kids had been in possession of her SUV until ditching it, according to the news.

Before closing the door, he poked his head outside and took a look around to see if anyone had been watching, but the street was empty. He eased the door shut and locked it. As he turned around, he saw Noreen removing the black scarf from her head. There were many flecks of blood in her hair, as well as more on her chin and on the part of her chest visible above the neckline of her black dress. The dress itself was also heavily bloodstained. The sight of it brought home the dire reality of all that had happened in a way nothing else could.

"Noreen—"

Her hand came arcing toward him so fast the motion of it was a nearly imperceptible blur, but he felt the heavy impact as her palm whipped across his face so hard it made him stagger away from her. He saw her coming again and held up a hand in a feeble gesture of defense, but she swatted it away and punched him in the throat, dropping him to his knees. The blow made him gag and feel incapable of breathing for a few moments. She grabbed him by an arm and dragged him into the living room, throwing him down on the white sofa. He tried to sit up, but she forced him onto his back and climbed atop him, straddling him.

There was little time for thought as all this violence was occurring. All he knew in those moments was a combination of pure terror and utter astonishment at her brutal display of incredible strength. He was no tough guy, but he wasn't a total weakling either. There was no shortage of men who could kick his ass, but not many could have physically overpowered him with such speed and ease.

She locked her hands around his throat and spent several moments choking him, stopping only after his thoughts turned fuzzy and his vision began to blur. His bladder released, staining his pants with piss. He was crying when she started slapping him again, bringing him back to full consciousness.

Noreen smiled in a savage way once she saw he was alert again. "The one-eyed man told me you did this, Elliot. You're the reason my kids are on the run, why I don't know where they're at right now.

You're the reason I've had to kill people today and can now never return to my home. I am very angry with you. Do you know that?"

He blubbered pathetically without being able to utter coherent words.

The answer was obvious anyway.

Her hands returned to his throat, but this time she didn't squeeze. "There's no use denying anything. I already know you betrayed us, but I want to hear it from you. Give me your coward's confession, Elliot. I want to know all of it, how it happened and why."

He sniffled and blinked away tears. "Are you a daywalker too?"

She laughed. "Of course, you fucking idiot. Now talk."

He drew in a ragged breath and shuddered. "What's the point? You're just going to kill me anyway."

Noreen smiled. "Maybe." There was a strangely playful lilt to her voice now. "And maybe not. The one-eyed man told me you did it for love. He said you've always been in love with me." She shrugged, still smiling. "So tell me your story. Convince me you're worthy of my love and maybe you get to live after all. Maybe we can run off somewhere together, just you and me." Her thumbs pressed into the hollow of his throat, making him wince. "Or keep quiet and die in certain agony when I rip out your throat."

The pressure of her thumbs against his soft flesh increased slightly more.

"Okay, okay!" came his sputtering response. "I'll tell you everything. Just please stop choking me. It hurts."

He whimpered.

She relaxed the pressure on his throat and sat back slightly. "All right. Like I said, this is your chance. Your one and only ever chance. Explain yourself."

Elliot grunted and shifted uncomfortably beneath her for a moment.

Then he started talking, telling her all of it, just as she'd demanded.

Starting with how, in the beginning, when he was still feeling things out and wasn't yet sure he could go through with ratting out his best friend, he'd been so cautious. His initial contacts with members of the organization of hunters were tentative and non-committal. He had several conversations with two men that got longer with each subsequent one that occurred. There was one man who went by the name of Anton. He was the more aggressive and persistent of the two, constantly pushing him for more details about the vampire he knew, but Elliot remained reticent, speaking at length but only in vague terms rather than specifics. Anton became increasingly angry, warning him that he was dealing with dangerous people and that he should be wary of the consequences of jerking them around.

The implied threat rattled Elliot enough to consider abandoning further pursuit of the betrayal he'd long contemplated. At that point he was still uncertain of the organization, doubtful of their trustworthiness and worried they were just crackpots playing at being the kind of vampire hunters they'd seen on television.

He'd learned of the organization in the first place by researching the subject online. This was not long after Jonathan had drunkenly divulged his secret nature. At first he only encountered useless forums and blogs related to vampire role-playing games, but in the off-topic section of one such forum he encountered an intriguingly cryptic post about "real" monsters. A link in that post sent him down a dizzyingly steep internet rabbit hole that ended with him procuring contact information for members of a network of supposedly genuine monster trackers and hunters.

He ceased his research not long after Jonathan disappeared, believing fate had granted him an easier way to earn Noreen's affections. She'd been the object of his sexual obsession for so long. Several months passed with no hint of her husband ever returning. Elliot had been convinced she would need a comforting shoulder to lean on, but she'd seemed oblivious to all his awkward advances.

Frustration caused him to take up his research again and, eventually, he renewed his contact with members of the organization of hunters. Discussions of greater depth ensued.

Despite the intensity of his obsession with Noreen, he'd sought further reassurance that he was doing the right thing. He also wanted a guarantee that no harm would come to the family of the vampire he was turning over. An in-person meeting was arranged with the organization's regional boss. They talked things out over a lunch Elliot barely touched at a diner in another town. The man had a trim build and wore a suit that made him look more like a businessman than a hunter of monsters. His name was Mr. McCabe. Elliot knew this in advance because Anton had told him on the phone. A first name was never provided.

McCabe spoke in the polished language and tone of a Manhattan advertising executive. He had a lot to say about the nobility of his organization and the work it did to make the world a safer place.

Work that would never earn the men and women he employed the recognition they deserved. He was such a smooth talker that just listening to him made Elliot feel better. His remaining reticence faded to nothing over the course of that lunch. McCabe gave his word that no one other than the vampire he was outing would be hurt.

He spilled everything, including a sincere and tearful profession of his love for Noreen.

McCabe smiled and nodded at this revelation, as if sexual desire was a perfectly valid reason for betrayal.

Because the vampire was missing, the family would have to be approached and interrogated, but the man gave his word they would not be harmed. The lunch ended and the two men parted ways after shaking hands.

Weeks passed with no contact from the organization.

Until today.

A one-eyed man attired in black showed up at his door around noon, on Elliot's lunch break. He knew as soon as he heard the man talk that it was Anton. The hunter pushed past him into his house and informed him he would personally be visiting the Murphys that very day to extract the necessary information. He also told Elliot he should expect a call later that afternoon, after the mission was complete.

Thus began one of the tensest, most nerve-wracking experiences of Elliot's life as he stayed at home and awaited word from the one-eyed man instead of returning to work. Hours passed and his phone mostly remained silent, save for the occasional text from co-workers and spammers.

Then came the first news reports of a violent disturbance at a house in Noreen's neighborhood. At first he didn't think it was connected to the one-eyed man's visit to her house. He'd convinced himself that nothing more than perhaps a slightly uncomfortable chat would occur, certainly nothing that could lead to day-long breathless news coverage. Then he saw the first exterior shot of her house on the local ABC affiliate and knew something disastrous had occurred, that all his worst fears about how things could go had not only come true, they'd been exceeded in terrible ways he'd never imagined.

"I'm so sorry," he told her, sniffling as he arrived at the end of his account. "You have to believe me. I never meant for any of this to happen. If I'd known it would come to this—if I'd even suspected— I never would've gone through with it. I would've talked to you.

Warned you."

Noreen's expression turned hard. "But you didn't."

His whimpering resumed and for some moments he again struggled to speak intelligibly, until finally squeezing out, "Please. You have to forgive me."

Noreen's hands locked around his throat again.

She leaned in close, to a point just shy of their lips touching. Her eyes were gorgeous, mesmerizing. Even under the threat of death, he found himself entranced by her beauty and still so desperately in love.

She whispered, "No."

She pushed her thumbnails into the hollow of his throat, driving them through the flesh as easily as she'd push them through cookie dough. The hole she created was small at first, but blood jetted from it anyway, leaping high enough for Elliot to see it strike her chin. Her thumbs dug deeper and deeper, his blood painting her face red. Instinct caused him to struggle even though he knew it was hopeless. She laughed at his struggles and lapped at his blood.

She drank for several more moments before unleashing a scream of rage. Then she gripped the sides of his head and tore it free of his body, tossing it away from her. The neck stump of Elliot's head hit the television, leaving a crimson smear on the screen as it fell to the floor. Noreen looked at the screen and saw a reporter on the scene at the convenience store in Lakemoor talking through a mask of trickling blood.

She screamed again.

TWENTY-FOUR

A LARGE MAIN ROOM ENCOMPASSED the bulk of the cabin's first floor square footage, with the rest left over for the small kitchen in back and an adjacent half-bathroom. A section of the main room was set up in the standard manner of a living room in a typical suburban house, with seating in the form of recliners and a couch, all arranged so they were facing the large wall-mounted television. The difference was there were no walls sectioning off this area from the rest of the first floor. The only bedrooms were upstairs, as was the cabin's only full bathroom.

Another portion of the large, open downstairs space had been set aside as a rec-room type of area. It was dominated by a professional quality billiards table. A rack of cue sticks was affixed to the nearest wall. Also mounted to the wall was a cabinet that, when opened, revealed a dart board inside, a fancy one that looked like it belonged in an English pub. Closer to one of the covered windows at the front of the cabin was a round dining table, one Zach figured was primarily used for tabletop gaming. The guess was based on the proximity of bookshelves filled with old staples like Monopoly, Clue, and Trivial Pursuit, along with somewhat more modern selections such as Catan and Cards Against Humanity.

Zach had deposited the bulk of their weapons stash on the table's surface. The stash included two AR-15s, a shotgun, a bolt-action rifle with scope attached, multiple handguns, a katana in a leather sheath, a couple of the most lethal-looking knives he'd ever seen, and a crossbow. There was also a shitload of ammunition, some piled on the surface and another crate stashed underneath it.

The big question on Zach's mind as he explored the interior of the cabin was the matter of who all the recreational stuff was for. Their mother couldn't possibly have spent much time up here, at least not at any point in the recent past. It was obvious Jonathan Murphy had been here at some point, but it was far from clear how long ago. Even if he'd stopped by recently, a prolonged stay seemed unlikely. The risk of being discovered here by his scorned wife might've been a slight one, but it was still a risk. She could show up at any point looking for him, and a man who'd worked so hard to stay hidden probably wouldn't take that chance.

Probably being the operative word.

All that was without even considering who else might be looking for him, people who might eventually find their way to a cabin he owned despite it being purchased under a false identity. It was hard to guess what might really be going through his father's mind these days. He still had no real insight into what had driven the man's decision to desert them. That he'd been up to some shady shit was obvious. Not only that, but the shady shit had clearly been going on for a long time and had involved his wife as well.

Trying to figure any of it out without a lot of additional information was an exercise in futility. It was also kind of making his head hurt, or maybe that was just an effect of the strong beers his father had left behind. He'd had two and couldn't help noticing they made him drunker than he'd feel from double the amount of ordinary domestic beers. His experience with booze was limited, being still a few years removed from legal age, but he knew enough to realize he needed to cut himself off now. Having one or two to relieve tension was okay, but he wanted a clear head in case things got crazy again.

He just wished there were beverages in the fridge other than beer, but there was nothing. Well, there was also the blood. He guessed blood counted as a beverage if you were a vampire, but he was just an ordinary human kid with ordinary drink preferences.

This was on his mind as he returned to the kitchen and pulled the refrigerator door open, frowning again at its puzzling contents. Seconds later, he threw the door shut, frustration causing him to use much greater force than necessary. Hearing a noise from inside the appliance, he opened the door again and saw that by slamming it he'd caused one of the blood pouches on the top shelf to slide off the pile. The bag wound up caught between one of the door compartments and the middle shelf, but now it dropped out of the fridge to the floor.

He knelt to snatch up the bag, but it was slick to the touch and slipped from his fingers, plopping down on the floor again. This time it landed a couple of feet to his right. He moved to pick it up again, but in his haste he miscalculated and stepped on the bag. It yielded to his weight, blood erupting from it as it split open. He heard the television turn on in the main room in nearly the same instant and guessed Chelsea had found the remote. An ad for a car rental agency was playing. The channel changed and he heard a female reporter talking in excited tones.

About them, of course.

Zach started hunting around the kitchen for cleaning materials, but he saw nothing, not even a dish rag near the sink. There was what looked like a small closet next to the open bathroom door, but its door was closed. There might be stuff he could use in there, perhaps even a mop and bucket, but the bottom of his shoe was soaked in blood. He didn't see how he could avoid making an even bigger mess without calling Chelsea into the kitchen.

He looked at the back door, the one that led out to the parking area behind the cabin. It was only a few feet away. He could step out there and scuff his shoe against the ground until he'd gotten it clean enough to not leave a trail of bloody footprints all over the cabin when he went back inside. His hand was on the doorknob and already in the process of turning it when he thought to take a peek outside first.

This time inside the cabin was the closest they'd come to experiencing peace all day, but he couldn't start letting his guard down. He pulled back an edge of the curtain and grimaced when he saw a tall man in a black suit standing in the parking area, staring at the back of the cabin with an unreadable expression. Seeing him back there gave Zach quite a shock, making him gasp and let go of the doorknob.

The man had limp gray hair that hung to the collar of his white shirt. He had a gaunt, almost emaciated appearance, with thin, bloodless lips and skin that looked ashen. His mouth was open and he didn't appear to blink. The sight of the strange man was so unnerving that several moments passed before something else of importance registered. The shed's door had been busted open. A padlock dangled from the hasp, which was bent out of shape but still attached to the jamb.

Zach would not have guessed the man capable of exerting anywhere near that level of strength. He was so thin and looked so frail, almost insubstantial, like he could be carried away by a strong gust of wind. The shed's door had been broken open from within, not from the outside. This struck him as inconceivable and impossible to understand until he remembered what he'd glimpsed through those dirty double windows.

The coffins.

He couldn't help flashing back to their grisly discovery in the storage unit. Another coffin, one with a body inside it. This man was no rotting corpse, but he did look sort of dead anyway, like one of the walking ghouls from *Night of the Living Dead*. It seemed unlikely he'd been slumbering in one of the coffins, but it was hard to fully dismiss the idea on a day already filled to the brim with preposterous and unlikely things.

Assuming he'd indeed broken out of the shed, it stood to reason someone else had locked him inside it. Zach's father might have done it, maybe even his mother. This was their property, they'd owned it for many years, according to what he'd been told today. What he couldn't understand was how the man could have survived a protracted period of imprisonment in the shed without starving or dying of thirst. Surely at some point he would've become desperate enough to escape by breaking out the double windows in back, which had to be an easier way out than smashing open a bolted door.

He was again contemplating wild thoughts of vampires and other otherworldly things when the white-faced ghoul took a step toward the cabin. The sudden forward movement elicited a louder gasp from Zach and caused him to take some rapid steps backward. His feet started sliding out from under him just as he remembered the blood all over the floor. He made a vain attempt to recover his balance, flailing his arms about briefly before flopping backward and landing hard on his ass.

His sister heard the loud crash and called out his name in a panicked voice. He heard her come running even as he rolled over and scrambled back to his feet, still sliding in the wide pool of blood. Chelsea appeared in the open doorway and gaped at him, undoubtedly aghast at the bloody scene. His shirt was covered in blood and his hands were dripping with it. He was sure he looked like a mad-dog killer caught red-handed at the scene of his latest crime, but it didn't matter. He didn't have time to explain anything, which was why he brushed past Chelsea and ran into the main room, making a beeline for the table of weapons.

He grabbed the Glock-19 for the simple reason that it was loaded and he already knew how to use it. The gun slipped from his fingers and hit the floor, the slick, wet blood coating his fingers loosening his grip on it.

"Goddammit!"

He wiped his hand on the seat of his pants, scooped the gun up again, and ran back into the kitchen. The whole time Chelsea was following him around and shouting questions at him. He could tell she was getting irritated by his failure to respond, but he only had room in his head just then for dealing with the immediate threat of the ghoul from the shed.

After once again nearly slipping in the spreading pool of blood on the floor, he opened the back door, kicked open the screen door on the other side, and stepped outside, aiming the Glock in front of him in a two-handed grip.

He frowned.

The tall, ashen-looking man in the rumpled suit was gone.

He experienced a moment of intense confusion before arriving at the obvious conclusion. Having found the back door locked, the strange man had gone around to the front of the cabin to try his luck there.

Chelsea stepped out onto the porch as he descended the steps to the ground. "Zach, what the hell is going on? Have you lost your mind?"

He shot a quick glance over his shoulder. "Go back inside and lock the door. There's someone out here."

She frowned as she took a look around. "I don't see anybody."

"I think he went around to the front. Now get the fuck back inside while I check it out." His tone was curt, tinged with exasperation, a feeling that deepened when he turned and looked fully at her. She still hadn't moved. "Are you even listening to me?"

She scowled. "I appreciate the concern, but I can handle myself just as well as you. Maybe better. Or have you forgotten?"

Fuck it.

There simply wasn't time to argue with her.

He'd started moving toward the side of the cabin when he happened to glance at the shed again and saw something that stopped him in his tracks. Something that made no sense, that just wasn't possible, not unless he now needed to answer in the affirmative to his sister's question about losing his mind.

The shed door was intact and shut.

The padlock hanging from the hasp was still securely in place.

Zach stood frozen there for several moments as he struggled to decide whether what he was seeing was real. Never at any previous point in his life had he experienced hallucinations, yet he could only come to one of two possible conclusions. Either he'd hallucinated the strange man and the busted-open door, or he was hallucinating right now. The latter was probably the more terrifying possibility, but each was deeply disturbing.

He let out a breath and started walking toward the shed, moving slowly and casting a wary glance around while still holding the gun out in front of him.

Chelsea trotted after him. "Okay, seriously, what's happening here?"

Zach's gaze locked on the shed door. "I don't know. Just give me a minute. I need to check something before I try to explain."

She sighed but said nothing.

The intact shed door didn't flicker in and out of existence like a movie depiction of a hallucination. It didn't change at all as he got closer and closer. He started shaking again once he was within a few feet of it. Chelsea put a hand lightly against his back, a comforting gesture, but again she said nothing, opting for patience now as he worked through what was troubling him.

He came to a stop as he arrived at the shed.

Then he let out another big breath, took one of his hands off the gun, and reached out to touch the door. He felt solid wood against his fingers, the rough grain of it prickly against his skin. Next he tested the bolt and the padlock. Both were solid, strong and sturdy, just like the door itself. Only a person imbued with a tremendous level of strength, some roided-up muscleman, would have any chance of smashing through it.

Shuddering, he turned away from the door and looked at Chelsea. "You're gonna think I'm crazy."

She rolled her eyes. "Do you really believe that? Think of

everything we've been through today. It's *all* fucking crazy. Just spill it."

He shrugged. "Okay."

He told her the whole thing. Every detail.

She was frowning hard by the time he finished. "You should have told me about the coffins."

"I guess so." There was a touch of reluctant contriteness in his voice. "I just didn't want to give you more to worry about."

She laughed, shaking her head. "We've both got plenty to worry about. What difference is one more fucking thing? You should've told me."

He nodded, fully accepting it now. "Yeah. You're right. I'm sorry. But what do we do now? Something out here made me see something that wasn't there. Should we really stay here?"

She groaned. "I don't know. I don't see how we have any choice. Cops everywhere are looking for us. We've got lots of guns and ammo and other shit to protect us here. Maybe there's something locked in one of those coffins that can somehow play tricks on our minds. Or maybe not. Who the fuck knows? But if there is, their power must be pretty limited or they would've gotten out of there a long time ago. So maybe keep the curtains shut and don't look out back."

Zach nodded again but said nothing.

He hoped she was right about the limited reach. He hoped whatever was locked in the shed wouldn't break out for real, because if that happened, he wasn't convinced all the guns and ammo in the world would be enough to keep them safe.

TWENTY-FIVE

MULTIPLE DISTRACTIONS HAD DELAYED NOREEN'S exit from her adopted hometown, but her end goal of reuniting with her kids remained the same. Yes, that goal had slipped from the forefront of her mind into the background at times, but it never retreated fully from her awareness. The problem was she was riding a rush from drinking far more fresh blood in a short period of time than she had at any point since the wild early days with Jonathan.

At the conclusion of a protracted torture session in the storage unit with the woman from the rental office, she'd had every intention of heading out to the interstate to begin the drive to Stillwater Lake. The problem was she'd become so freshly invigorated by what she'd done to the woman that it was hard to think of anything other than immediately doing it again. It'd been so long since she'd toyed with a helpless human for the sheer fun of it. Even the thing with Amelia had been very different. That'd been about revenge, something done in a frenzy of fury. This, instead, had been a form of play, albeit of a profoundly sadistic variety.

Back in the days before the kids and the extended experiment in suburban tranquility, she and Jonathan had frequently done similar things. They made a game of it, picking up young women and men from bars and luring them back to wherever they happened to be living at the time. There they would go through the early motions of initiating a sexual encounter, lulling the marks into a sense of mutual fun and safety before revealing the darker truth in the form of extensive and progressively more cruel exercises in degradation. The desperate begging and pleading before they died had always been Noreen's favorite part. She'd forgotten what a joy that was until today.

After leaving the storage facility, her thoughts returned to Elliot Valentine and the matter of his betrayal. The instant that happened, she knew she couldn't leave without paying him a visit. Of course, there was a chance he might not be home when she arrived, but that was okay. She would wait for him. Unless they chose to turn themselves in, the kids could only be headed to Stillwater Lake. The public scrutiny and law enforcement pressure had become too intense for anything else. She remained confident in eventually reuniting with them. It'd just take a little longer than she originally planned.

As it turned out, she didn't have to wait because Elliot was already home. She was pleased to find him there, but she wound up not playing with him as extensively as she'd hoped, primarily because, as with Amelia, she'd been overcome with rage. He'd transgressed against her—against her entire family—and he had to pay. The intense terror and overwhelming remorse she'd read in his expression as she'd torn open his throat was satisfaction enough. She'd entertained the notion of turning him, transforming him into a thing the hunters he'd conspired with would want to exterminate. There would have been a twisted form of dark poetry in such an act, but in the end the impulse was overwhelmed by a greater desire to destroy him utterly.

Once she was finished with him, she realized she could not immediately leave his house. Though it was early evening by then and the sun had begun its slow descent toward the horizon, it was still daylight out. She was covered in blood. Her black dress was crimson-soaked and her hair was thick with it. She checked and, unsurprisingly, found no women's clothing items in Elliot's house. Nor were there any clothes of his she found acceptable.

She stripped off the dress and spent some time blotting up blood with a damp cloth before further treating it with a sponge and hydrogen peroxide. This was a painstaking exercise that took more time than she would've liked, but it was not, in her opinion, enough. After doing all she could with it, she threw the garment in Elliot's washing machine. She waited until it was done in the wash, then transferred it to the dryer. It was at that point that she again took a shower for the purpose of cleansing blood from her body. Having to do it for a second time in one day made her think again of the old days with Jonathan. This brought a momentary warm rush of nostalgia that was quickly replaced once again by rage. It was Jonathan's fault all this was happening, and one way or another she would have her revenge against him, just as she had with Elliot.

All the while as these things were happening, she remained aware of time passing. It started to get darker outside. She turned on more lights in the house and occasionally got up from the couch to check on the dryer. An underlying feeling of guilt for taking so long to get on the road to Stillwater Lake made her slightly fretful, but not enough to rush things.

Once she was finally ready to leave, she grabbed her handbag and the keys she'd taken from Amelia and headed outside, leaving the front door open a crack as she took long, quick strides across the lawn to the street. She kept her head down until she was inside the BMW.

She drove off down the street at a speed several miles above the posted low neighborhood limit. Not recklessly fast, but faster than was probably advisable with witnesses around. She couldn't help it. Part of it was an anxious need to belatedly begin the journey to Stillwater Lake, but probably more of it was the jittery over-amped feeling that came with an extreme level of overindulgence. The feeling had been with her for hours now, intensifying rather than leveling off because she hadn't had the good sense to stop after fully draining the one-eyed man. It made her feel strong and invincible and she liked that, but it also greatly increased the likelihood of making rash, impulsive mistakes and bad decisions.

She was on edge as she drove through the town, worried she'd be recognized by a cop or civilian before she could reach the interstate. Blue lights suddenly flashing behind her would've been about the least surprising thing ever, but to her amazement she reached the interstate without incident.

She was around ten miles down the road to Stillwater Lake when she realized she was being followed. At first she wasn't sure, thinking maybe it was more blood mania fueling an overly elevated level of paranoia. In an attempt to allay her fears, she experimented with speeding up and changing lanes, then changing lanes again. The driver of the black Mercedes was mildly subtle in his technique, refraining from precisely matching her speed and waiting a few moments each time before changing lanes, but he stayed with her.

She supposed it was possible he believed she was too frazzled to worry about any vehicle not obviously connected with law enforcement. She couldn't tell much about the person behind the wheel of the Mercedes at the average distance the driver was maintaining, except that he was almost certainly a man. He might have chauvinist tendencies causing him to doubt her perceptiveness. As in all things involving men, Noreen was inclined to believe the worst of him. She hoped she was right, because in this case it'd probably work to her advantage.

Instead of engaging in more evasion tactics, she slid into the right-hand lane and drove on at a moderate speed for another dozen miles. Long enough, she hoped, to lull the pursuer into believing she wasn't onto him. During that time, she gave some thought to who he might be. It was possible he was a plainclothes cop hoping she'd lead him to her kids. In that case, there might be more unmarked vehicles trailing behind him. Or maybe it was yet another person from the organization of hunters. She decided the person's identity ultimately did not matter. Either way, it didn't change what she knew she had to do.

A rest area was coming up on the right. When she was within fifty yards of the exit, she hit her blinker and slowed the BMW's speed. She kept her head still and facing forward but allowed her eyes to flick toward the rearview mirror several times as she continued to decelerate. The driver of the Mercedes did not put on his blinker, perhaps a last nod toward deflecting attention and suspicion, but the vehicle was noticeably slowing. She was not surprised to see it veer off the interstate and into the exit lane behind her.

She drove the rest of the way along the looping exit lane at a moderate, appropriate speed, soon pulling into the parking lot outside the rest area building. There were two long, opposing rows of parking spaces, one right in front of the building, the other at the back of the lot. About a third of the spaces were occupied as Noreen drove slowly past the front of the building. She opted for a space in front but off to the side a little, reaching for her handbag after cutting the BMW's engine and putting the car in park.

Before getting out, she checked her mirror again and saw the Mercedes had parked in the back row of spaces. The driver had backed in, leaving the vehicle's front end facing the building and the wide gap between rows of parking spaces.

Noreen smirked.

Getaway posture.

The son of a bitch really was underestimating her. It galled her to know he likely thought he could succeed where his associates had failed so spectacularly, but she pushed her anger down as she got out of the car, not even glancing at the Mercedes as she entered the building and went to the ladies' room.

She walked up to the long wash basin opposite the row of stainless-steel stalls. A few of the stalls were closed, but most of the doors were open wide enough to see they were unoccupied. Someone in one of the closed stalls had her phone out and seemed to be watching a clip of some bubble-brained YouTube influencer. The volume was obnoxiously loud for a space of this type. This wasn't a bathroom at a nightclub. It was a nexus of anonymity, a place where a steady and unending flow of strangers wordlessly crossed paths briefly before disappearing from each other's lives forever. The noise was intrusive to the point of distraction and once again she experienced a strong urge to lash out and kill without regard to whether she should.

Instead she set her bag next to one of the sinks on the basin and looked at the mirror, checking the makeup she'd applied before leaving Elliot's house. She thought it looked okay, not that she cared overly much. It was just something to do, a delaying tactic as she played the waiting game with the man in the Mercedes. She figured if she waited long enough he'd become impatient and enter the building. If he got close enough to the ladies' room, she might be able to drag him inside and rip his throat out while locked in one of the stalls. It'd be risky, but she badly wanted the interloper out of the equation so she could drive the rest of the way to Stillwater Lake in peace.

A toilet flushed and the YouTube clip abruptly ceased playing. A stall opened and a beautiful blonde woman in perfect makeup and strappy heels approached the basin. She was wearing an expensive-looking dress of shimmering turquoise. It was an outfit made for clubbing, which jived with her earlier thoughts about the woman before even seeing her. What she was doing in a public rest area many miles from any place where attire like this was appropriate, she had no idea.

The woman set her purse on the sink near Noreen's much larger bag. She was annoyed by the woman's proximity and considered spending some time shut away in one of the stalls, but then she noticed how the woman was staring into the open top of her bag. Big eyelashes fluttered at the sight of the blood bags and the guns.

She locked eyes with Noreen.

A spark of recognition occurred. The woman slapped a hand over her mouth as it opened wide, taking a backward step. Noreen glanced at the mirror. Two stalls were still closed, presumably with women still inside them, but no one else was in the open area outside the stalls. Knowing she had only seconds to operate before that changed, she grabbed one of the guns and smacked the butt of it against the woman's temple hard enough to fracture her skull. She caught her in her arms before she could fall to the floor and dragged her into one of the open stalls, breaking her neck after shutting the door.

She was dead.

After ensuring she'd arranged the woman in such a way that she wouldn't easily slide off the toilet, she turned to leave, but stopped when she heard another toilet flush. One of the other stalls opened. Noreen put an eye to the gap between the door and frame of the stall she was sharing with her latest victim, watching as a plump older woman in pink shorts and a "What happens in Vegas stays in Vegas" shirt washed her hands at the basin. The woman glanced at the handbags that had been left there in a curious way, causing Noreen to worry she'd immediately have to kill yet again.

Instead the woman walked out of the bathroom after drying her hands, leaving the bags alone. The moment she was gone, Noreen rushed to the basin and retrieved the handbags. Hearing the bathroom door open, she rushed back into the stall and locked herself inside.

Noreen stayed right where she was for a considerable period, sitting carefully on the lap of the dead woman so as not to dislodge her. She lost track of how many women came and went from the ladies' room as the steady stream of transitory highway travelers went on and on. At last there came a time when she was reasonably certain she had the space to herself.

She crawled out through the gap beneath the door in order to leave it locked behind her. At least an hour had passed since she'd entered the bathroom. She'd grown weary of playing the waiting game with the Mercedes man and had become more achingly conscious of how long she was dragging out the potential reunion with her kids.

After one more cursory check of herself in the large mirror over the basin, she opened the door to the ladies' room and took a careful look around at the building's lobby. She hadn't gotten a close look at the man from the Mercedes, but she was sure he wasn't here. No one was watching her or acting in a suspicious manner.

She moved quickly through the lobby, pushed open the door, and stepped outside. Off to her right was a young family struggling with an uncooperative vending machine. Beyond where they were, an older couple was sitting at a picnic table. There were fewer cars in the lot now. Once again, she had no sense of anyone watching her or behaving strangely.

Noreen walked up to the sidewalk and stared at the space where the Mercedes had been.

It was gone.

She slowly scanned the entire lot, but there was no sign of it.

So now she wondered whether she'd been overreacting all along. Maybe the man in the Mercedes hadn't been following her at all. She wanted to believe that, but something inside her, some deep, primitive instinct, wasn't buying it. She hadn't imagined the deliberate way he'd kept up with her, even if he'd been somewhat subtle about it. It wouldn't be smart to assume he'd simply abandoned the chase. She had a feeling she'd be seeing that sleek black car again, but it was something she could worry about later.

She got in the BMW and headed back out to the interstate.

TWENTY-SIX

A SURPRISING REVELATION STRUCK CHELSEA as she flipped through all the channels showing news coverage of the events in Lakemoor and her hometown. Even after having spent hours existing in sheer desperation mode, it was still possible to become bored in a supposedly safe haven after a relatively short time.

Part of the problem was social disengagement. Not having her phone—the good one—meant she was disconnected from her network of friends and acquaintances. The burner phone she'd been using was a poor substitute, but knowing she could in theory use it to log into her social accounts made her squirm with restless anxiety. It'd almost be better to have no phone at all, removing even the remotest possibility of doing something so reckless.

She frowned as she continued to stew over it and flip again and again through the same rotation of channels. The lack of new developments in the case meant the reporters were stuck in a rut of endlessly regurgitating the things they'd already said countless times. The number of live location spots had decreased markedly, with previously recorded segments now dominating coverage. One of the local stations had even abandoned continuous coverage altogether, switching over to a regularly scheduled game show. She had a feeling it wouldn't be much longer before the others followed suit.

This was a good thing for them. It meant that against all odds they'd succeeded in their longshot quest to slip away and get to a place of relative safety without being recognized or captured. Somewhere around an hour and a half had passed since their arrival at the cabin and so far no cops or anyone else had shown up looking for them. Chelsea felt relieved and grateful for these things, but she nonetheless wished for some small deviation in the repetitive news coverage. Some new tidbit of information about Mom, perhaps, or some new statement from the police, anything new at all, but nothing of the sort happened.

When a second local station suspended its coverage of the story, Chelsea decided she would try distracting herself by watching something entirely unrelated, maybe a movie or show. She began a slow scroll through all the channels available through the streaming TV provider, but nothing caught her fancy.

As she scrolled the channels, she reflected on how insane it was to feel this bored. All the drama and danger they'd made it through earlier in the day was one thing, but her brother seemed to have experienced a genuine supernatural event. She would have scoffed at hearing anything like it from anyone else, figuring the person relating the event to her was either a liar or a delusional mental case. There was a lot she still didn't understand about what had happened today, but she knew for a rock-solid fact he'd not made any of it up. It just wasn't something he would do, not for any reason.

Zach seemed to be doing his best to avoid thinking about the ghoul he'd hallucinated. He hadn't broached the subject at all since coming back into the cabin. It was almost as if he believed the strange phenomenon would fade into non-existence if they simply refused to acknowledge it. He'd been silent a while now, engaged in his own act of distraction, having found a thick old almanac from somewhere. He was reading it at the round dining table, and every now and then she heard him turning the pages.

Chelsea clicked back to the lone local station still covering the story. A reporter in a studio was talking, a female anchor who now seemed far more animated than she had the last time Chelsea checked the channel. The reason for her renewed excitement became clear a moment later.

Chelsea gasped.

Her heart felt like it skipped a beat as the on-screen image cut to a shot of the bullet-riddled GTO. The footage had been recorded earlier in the day when the sun was still out, but a new development was being discussed. Chelsea leaned forward on the sofa and turned the volume up higher.

An off-screen reporter said, "Shortly after emergency crews arrived on the scene, 21-year-old Austin Wheeler was transported to a nearby hospital. He sustained two reportedly non-life-threatening bullet wounds in the terrifying roadside incident. The young man is alert and speaking with authorities, and we can now reveal that he gave a brief statement to reporters at the hospital."

The on-screen image shifted again, this time to the scene just outside the entrance to a hospital emergency room. An ambulance had pulled up with lights flashing. Two EMTs unloaded a stretcher from the back and began to wheel it toward the emergency entrance. Police officers rushed into the shot, shouting at the reporters and camera operators to get back. The news crews made only the most minimal effort to comply, shouting questions to Austin Wheeler as the EMTs neared the entrance.

Chelsea glanced over at her brother. "Zach, check it. It's the guy from the GTO."

Zach turned another page in the almanac. Her words had not registered. She couldn't imagine what could possibly be so enthralling about an outdated Almanac, but she didn't bother trying to get his attention a second time. The time it'd take could cause her to miss something important.

She gasped again as her attention returned to the television.

The news crews had followed the stretcher and the EMTs into the lobby of the emergency room, but now something far more unusual was happening. Austin Wheeler was sitting up on the stretcher and demanding to address the reporters, fighting off the medical personnel urging him to lie back down. He fought so fiercely that at last they acquiesced.

The young man looked straight into the nearest camera and grinned, a surreal sight considering he had two bullets in him. His hair was short and slicked back with some kind of grease. He was good-looking but had an arrogant cast to his lean features, a corner of his mouth curling cockily in the manner of a young Elvis or James Dean.

"Hey, ya'll, my name is Austin Wheeler, and I want to state for the record that I am an innocent victim. One of the boys riding with me in the ambulance showed me a picture of those crazy kids on his phone, and I sure as heck recognized that little girl. Last time I saw her pretty face, she was aiming a pistol at me. Chelsea Murphy is a coldhearted black widow bitch, a mad dog in need of putting down. I sure as heck hope the po-po catches up with her soon, before she hurts any other innocent people."

Chelsea seethed as she listened to the man's self-serving speech. She clutched hard at the edges of the sofa cushions, digging her nails in deep in an attempt to keep from losing control. Hearing the person who'd chased her so relentlessly portray himself as an innocent victim was so galling and offensive she almost physically couldn't stand it. She wanted to leap through the big screen and strangle the smug asshole until his skin turned blue and his eyes bugged out.

On the screen, Wheeler turned his head again slightly, the smirk on his face deepening as he seemed to look right at her.

He chuckled. "I see you sitting there, little Chelsea, shaking like a leaf on a tree. Thinking your angry thoughts. That's a nice-looking cabin. Be a shame if some big, bad wolf was to come along and blow your door down."

Chelsea's eyes opened wide in alarm as she jumped up from the sofa and pointed at the screen. She yelled at the top of her lungs, desperate to finally snag her brother's attention. Someone else needed to see this and verify that she hadn't lost her grip on reality because all indications were that Wheeler could see her and was talking to her through the screen.

The sense of mind-bending desperation only relinquished its grip on her when she realized a trick was being played on her, one likely originating from the same mysterious force that had caused Zach to hallucinate earlier. A lengthy period of time had passed since that incident, lulling her into a false sense of safety. It'd been foolish to think they could escape its influence by merely moving to the front of the cabin. The beginning of the breaking news report about Wheeler might have been real, but what she was seeing and hearing now was only an illusion, one fed by her fears and the traumas she'd endured.

Recognizing this should have broken the spell. That was the way it'd seemed to work with her brother. Yet Wheeler was still looking right at her, licking his lips as he eyed her in a sleazily lascivious way that made her skin crawl. She glanced over her shoulder at Zach, who was still sitting at the table and paging through the almanac, apparently oblivious to her plight. Was it possible he somehow hadn't heard her screams? She didn't know how that could be, but it was the only thing that made sense. He would not deliberately ignore her sounds of distress. She loudly cried out for his attention again, but he never glanced her way.

Austin Wheeler's sinister laughter filled the room.

"I'm gonna have you all to myself soon, little Chelsea, and I'm gonna do so many fun things to your hot little body. Wicked, evil things. Gonna make you beg for mercy and cry out for more right after. You hear me, bitch? I'm gonna hear my name when I make you scream in passion and pain."

Chelsea closed her eyes. "This isn't happening. You're not really there."

Wheeler's voice boomed like thunder through the surround sound system. "*Look at me!*"

She felt weak and pitiful yielding to the forcefulness in that malevolent voice, but she was unable to help it, the fluttering of her eyelids a reflex reaction to terror. When they opened fully, she screamed again, because Wheeler appeared to be physically emerging through the screen, the upper half of his body protruding like the most realistic 3D movie image she'd ever seen. He had a switchblade knife in one hand and was grinning more broadly now, flashing fangs dripping saliva at the corners of his mouth.

Chelsea screamed and reeled backward, falling onto the sofa again as the upper half of Wheeler's body loomed high in the air above her. She jumped up and ran to the cabin's front door, thinking only of getting outside and far away from the impossible specter. She gripped the knob in both hands and twisted it fiercely, but it refused to turn.

A voice spoke and she screamed again.

The voice spoke again, its tone sharper this time. Only then did recognition pierce the terror consuming her. She let go of the doorknob and spun about, pressing her back against the door as she saw her brother rise from the table and approach her with a worried look on his face.

She whimpered as he got closer. "We have to leave this place. There's something evil here. Some force playing tricks and messing with our heads." She pushed away from the door and grabbed him by the hand. "Please, you have to trust me. We can't stay here."

Zach gave her a sympathetic look tinged with confusion. His head swiveled slowly about as he searched the cabin's main room for signs of anything amiss. The look of confusion was still in place when he met her gaze again. "Where would we go? The whole world is looking for us, Chel."

The way she felt just then, being recognized or possibly apprehended was the last thing she cared about. "I don't know," she said, wiping tears from her face with a trembling hand. "I don't even care anymore. We just have to fucking leave before it gets us."

Zach frowned. "Before *what* gets us?"

She slapped a hand against his chest, startling him and causing him to lean backward. "*It*, Zach, *it!*" she screamed, slapping his chest again. "You know what I'm talking about. It's the same thing that happened to you."

An inkling of insight dawned on Zach's face, his features relaxing out of the look of confusion. "Oh. Okay. Something happened, right? Something I couldn't see. Tell me about it."

She first glanced at the TV, shuddering in relief to see only an insurance commercial on the screen. Though the rational side of her knew what she'd seen had only been an especially vivid and powerful illusion, she kept expecting Wheeler's three-dimensional image to rise out of the screen again and step into the room.

She wiped more tears away as she met Zach's gaze and told him all about what she'd seen. She was happy and relieved to see no evidence of skepticism in his expression. Then again, given what he'd experienced, it was exactly what she should have expected.

He sighed when she'd finished telling him about it. "Well, shit, I wish I'd known that was happening, but I bet even if I'd looked over there, I wouldn't have seen anything."

Chelsea nodded.

She had the same feeling.

She gripped him by the hand again. "Can we please go?"

Zach's shoulders slumped slightly, as if in defeat. "Yeah. This is too much. We're in so far over our heads we're drowning. Even without this weird-ass shit, I don't see how we could go on much longer. There's no food in this place. None anywhere. I looked all over. Nothing to drink but tap water and beer I don't want. There's, like, two rolls of fucking toilet paper in this place. Maybe we should just figure out where the nearest police station is and turn ourselves in."

The prospect of prison time was no more appealing than it had been prior to coming to the cabin, but Chelsea felt ready to face the consequences of their actions. In a way, it'd be a relief to relinquish control of her fate to a system rooted in hard reality and easily understood things.

She squeezed his hand. "Thank you. I—"

An excruciatingly painful abdominal spasm cut off her next words. She screeched in agony and let go of Zach's hand as she doubled over, opening her mouth wide and gagging as another, even more painful spasm seized her midsection. Her eyes filled with tears that stemmed not just from the pain but from a sense of extreme bitterness. The spasms were a recurrence of what she'd experienced on the interstate, only they were vastly more intense this time. Her guts were throbbing and squirming, and the waves of nausea that washed over her were so powerful they caused her to take a few staggering steps away from Zach and drop to her knees.

She heard her brother's urgent and increasingly desperate pleas to know what was happening, but she was incapable of responding. The pain was too overwhelming, the feeling of sickness too strong. Coherent speech was beyond her, her vocal cords useful only for producing sounds of immense suffering. Her tears flowed so freely they blurred her vision and dripped like water from a tap to the floor. Her back arched suddenly and she squealed loudly, like a wounded wild animal, as the worst spasm yet came, making her feel like she was on the verge of being torn apart. Her fingernails dug into the hardwood floor, bending and shredding as they scraped gouges in the varnish. Bile surged into her throat, making her gag again as she choked against the acidic burn. Her brother was screaming now too but his words barely registered. A faint, nearly inaudible sound of harsh laughter came from somewhere.

Did the sound come from her brother or Austin Wheeler?

Was it real or her imagination?

She couldn't tell.

She just knew she felt like she was dying.

In a fleeting instant of clarity, she heard Zach saying he would bring the car around to the front. He told her not to worry, that he'd be right back. Then they'd get out of this place and find a hospital. She couldn't say anything, couldn't even nod her agreement. All she could do was moan and pray for an end to her misery.

After imparting a last few words of reassurance, he started moving toward the kitchen, but stopped in his tracks when someone or something started pounding on the front door hard enough to make it vibrate in its frame. The person or creature on the other side of the door was making sounds that seemed not quite human. Roaring, frenzied sounds. Animal sounds. Like a starving bear desperately thrashing about while foraging for food. That would make sense, the cabin being surrounded by wilderness, but those pounding noises were incongruous. They sounded like they were being made by human fists, not by some unknown beast scratching and clawing.

Chelsea managed to lift her head and blink away enough of her tears to see her brother rush over to the round table. He grabbed the Glock again and positioned himself in front of the door with his arms extended, holding the gun in both hands.

He shouted a warning to whatever was on the other side of the door, telling it to go away before he blew its fucking head off. The pounding did not cease. If anything, it became more aggressive, the rattling of the door in the frame becoming louder and more disconcerting. The door was a heavy, solid slab of thick wood. It was difficult to imagine anything strong enough to smash it off its hinges, but it seemed close to happening anyway.

Zach shouted another warning.

His hands were shaking on the grip of the pistol.

The pounding continued, still growing in intensity. A loud cracking sound startled them both.

Zach squeezed the Glock's trigger.

The loud boom of the gun made Chelsea flinch. She flinched again as he squeezed the trigger a second time, and then a third. And then again and again, the bullets punching holes in the heavy wood as he emptied the gun's magazine.

There was a thump as something fell against the door.

The pounding had stopped.

Chelsea felt the suffocatingly tight band around her midsection loosen slightly.

Zach stood right where he was a few moments longer, still aiming the gun at the pockmarked door, his hands no longer shaking. He let out a breath, appearing to accept that the pounding would not resume. Then he went back over to the table, returned the Glock to its surface, and picked up another handgun, one that still had a full load in its magazine.

He gave Chelsea a curious look as he went to the door. "You mind if I take a look?"

She sat up as the waves of nausea continued to recede, wiping spittle and foam from her mouth. "I guess. Please be careful."

He nodded and unlocked the door, pulling it open only a crack at first, angling his gaze downward as he peered through it. There was no sharp gasp when he saw whatever was on the porch, counter to

Chelsea's expectations. Instead he stood there without moving or saying anything for an extended time, barely even seeming to breathe.

"What is it?" she asked him, becoming impatient.

Zach turned his head slowly toward her, confusion etched in his features as he pulled the door open and showed her the porch.

The empty, barren porch.

Still on her knees and feeling weak from the physical ravaging of the mystery sickness, she held out a hand and said, "Help me up."

Zach came over and grasped her hand, gently guiding her to her feet. She felt a little wobbly as she walked out to the porch with him, but the worst of the sickness had passed, leaving in its wake little in the way of aftereffects. By then she'd concluded this second episode was not a true continuation of what she'd experienced in the car. In that case, she'd inhaled some foul spore from the corpse in the coffin, perhaps just one little speck of contagion, leading to a sickness that'd already run its course. What she'd experienced this time, she was pretty sure, was instead supernatural manipulation, the malefic finger of a powerful force exploiting her previous trauma by tricking her into believing it was happening all over again.

It was twilight now, the sky a dark pencil-gray becoming perceptibly darker almost by the moment. The buzzing, chirping sounds of insects in the woods were more noticeable now than they'd been when they arrived. The inexorable approach of full night ignited a new tingling of dread in Chelsea. She wasn't sure which option made her more uneasy—being outside at night in this strange, unfamiliar place, or retreating back into the cabin, where they were at the mercy of the mysterious force.

For all she knew, that force could reach them even out here. They'd probably have to leave this area entirely to escape its influence. She still believed what Zach had proposed before the onset of the sickness was the smartest thing they could do. Just get in the car and drive away, then turn themselves in and be done with all this craziness.

She was about to say as much when she noticed the way her brother was intently studying the back of the door. At first she thought he was checking out the numerous exit holes made by the bullets he'd fired. They were slightly larger than the penetration points on the inside of the door, but as she followed his gaze and watched him touch the wood in several places, she realized that wasn't it at all. An inkling formed in her brain an instant before he turned toward her and said it.

"The only marks on this door are from the bullets. You heard what I heard, right? Some kind of monster was trying to bash its way in. There should be gouges in the wood, but there's just these fuckin' holes."

Chelsea looked at the back of the door again and shivered.

She didn't have to say what she was thinking, knowing they'd both already arrived at the same conclusion. The ferocious assault on the door had only happened in their minds. This time they'd shared a hallucinatory experience, a new wrinkle. It was possibly the most disturbing development yet because it meant they could be caught in the same malicious delusion without realizing it.

"Zach, let's just go. Now. Please."

He glanced at her, a numb look on his face as he nodded. "Okay."

They'd just started moving to the edge of the porch when the buzz of an approaching car engine became audible. Instead of going back inside and shutting the door, brother and sister stayed right where they were, listening as the sound of the engine steadily grew louder. The private drive was a long one, and unless the car they were hearing was coming up the drive, the sound should have diminished by now.

Instead it continued to get louder.

Chelsea sighed. "Do you think it's the cops?"

Zach shrugged. "Dunno. Not sure how they would know about this place, but I guess it's possible."

Chelsea frowned. "Or maybe Mom?"

Her brother shrugged again. "Could be, sure."

"Which would you rather?"

A hint of a smile touched his lips. "I honestly do not fucking know at this point."

Chelsea laughed because she felt the same way.

She glanced at the gun still gripped in his right hand, which was hanging down at his side now. "Should you put that away? What if it's the cops and they start blazing when they see you with a gun?"

Zach grunted. "I'll drop it the second I know it's them."

But it wasn't the cops.

A sleek black Mercedes came around the final bend in the tree-shrouded drive and rolled to a slow stop several feet from the porch. A middle-aged man with neatly trimmed salt-and-pepper hair was behind the wheel. Unless someone else was in the trunk or lying down in the backseat, he'd come alone.

The siblings glanced at each other.

Zach shrugged. So did Chelsea.

The man was a stranger.

The driver-side door came open and the man stepped out. He wore a tan trench coat over a suit and tie, not exactly ideal attire considering the humid conditions. Something in the way the garments fit his trim body so precisely gave the outfit the appearance of a second skin, in the sense that it became immediately impossible to imagine him in anything else. It was clearly an integral part of the way he presented himself to the world. Even without flashing a badge or any other official ID, he exuded the kind of quiet competence and authority that announced the arrival of a person ready to show up and take charge of any situation.

Zach raised the gun as the man approached the porch. "Stop right there. Who the fuck are you?"

The man came one step closer and stopped. "My name is Mr. McCabe, and I'm here to talk to you about your parents."

TWENTY-SEVEN

THE UNPLANNED LONG INTERLUDE AT the rest area weighed heavily on Noreen for the remainder of the drive up to Stillwater Lake. She'd thought she was being so clever with her waiting in the bathroom ploy, truly believing she could lure the mystery man into a position of vulnerability, but he hadn't come looking for her.

And Noreen wound up wasting over an hour sitting on the lap of a dead woman while locked inside a stall in the ladies' room. The man had departed at an indeterminate time prior to her emergence from the building, and it was the uncertainty about when he'd left that most worried her.

He might have driven away mere minutes before she walked back outside, or it might have happened almost right away, or at any point in between. It was impossible to know. She didn't know where he'd gone or whether he was even a real threat. It was still remotely possible she'd succumbed to paranoia and the man had no true interest in her at all. She still didn't really believe that was the case, though. He was an adversary, she was sure of it, and now he'd gained some important advantage over her.

She was unaccustomed to feeling this discomfited over anything, and it caused her to fret over her many missteps through the course of the day. Of even greater concern was how her kids perceived her now, in light of all the unsavory things they'd uncovered. She also feared how they would react if they were to learn of her true vampiric nature without being properly prepared in advance.

They might hate her.

Or recoil in revulsion.

The prospect of her kids feeling that way about her was depressing, but she had to be realistic. Many of their illusions had already been stripped away. The false impression that their sweet mother was an ordinary small-town housewife was gone, erased like an equation from a chalkboard. It was possible that in running off they'd hoped to never see her again.

She worried for their safety, but as the highway miles rolled away, she also felt an incipient anger. They were her kids, and kids were meant to obey their parents. It was the right and proper way of things. They belonged to her. They were her *property*. As such, her word was not to be defied. Whether they wanted it or not, she would be with them again, whatever it took. If they remained insolent and defiant, some form of punishment would be meted out. One way or another, they would fall in line.

And then everything would be all right again.

She was less than ten miles from the exit to Stillwater Lake when she heard the siren and glimpsed the flashing blue lights in her rearview mirror. The sudden whoop of the siren gave her a jolt. She hadn't been watching for police thanks to the singular and obsessive nature of her thoughts. At first she was confused as to why this was happening. She wasn't weaving all over the road and hadn't been cognizant of driving in any overtly reckless way. Then she looked at the speedometer and saw she was traveling a hair under 100 MPH, a speed more suitable for a racetrack than a two-lane highway.

Fuck.

Until that moment, she'd had no clue she was going anywhere near that fast, but she understood how it must have happened. She was consumed with anger and frustration, strong emotions her body expressed in a physical way by making her grip the wheel tighter and push the gas pedal to the floor while her oblivious brain seethed.

She cursed her shortsightedness and loss of control, knowing it'd put her in a perilous position. Not pulling over was not an option. A high-speed chase leading a parade of police cruisers up to the cabin at Stillwater Lake would not be ideal, to say the least.

Another, longer glance at the rearview mirror revealed that the officer in the cruiser behind her was patrolling without a partner, which made her feel marginally better. She'd have to hope she was only being pulled over for speeding. If the officer had recognized her, there was a real chance of her situation turning desperate in a hurry. In that case, he might not exit the cruiser at all, at least not at first. He might just sit back there and wait for backup. She was, after all, a major figure in an explosively violent series of incidents, starting with the grisly killing of the one-eyed man in her home.

Police everywhere were looking for her.

Well, maybe they'd found her.

She put on her blinker and slowly eased the BMW over to the breakdown lane. After putting the car in park, she lowered the driver-side window and let out a breath, trying to relax. She looked at the rearview mirror again and saw the cop staring at a screen on his dash and punching his fingers at a keyboard. Her gaze stayed on him the whole time, but he barely glanced at the BMW as he worked. At one point, he stopped what he was doing and leaned back slightly, putting a hand to his face in a thoughtful pose.

Then he shifted in his seat and stared directly at the rear of the BMW. His expression was unreadable, but the way he was just sitting there and staring made her uneasy. She began to think her guess about him waiting for backup might have been correct. Her fingers flexed around the steering wheel as her anxiety soared.

What was he doing back there?

What the fuck was he waiting for?

She feared the answers to those questions would not please her and gave some renewed thought to the notion of simply speeding away. There might yet be some slim chance of eluding him just long enough to ditch the car and slip away on foot. Unlikely, but she was starting to think it was a better chance than whatever was about to happen here. She'd refrained from turning the BMW's engine off in the event anything of the sort became necessary.

Her hand was beginning to drift toward the gear shifter when the cop surprised her by stepping out of the cruiser. She tensed again, her hand tightening on the shifter as she watched the man throw his door shut and stand near the edge of the road for a moment, watching the traffic go by. Then he hoisted his uniform trousers up a little higher and turned toward her, walking along the shoulder with a hand resting on the butt of his holstered pistol.

The hand on the gun worried her, but she was still hoping she could avoid serious consequences by playing the part of a frazzled, distracted woman guilty only of not paying adequate attention to her speed. The performance wouldn't be an entirely fictional one. She'd just have to amp up the ditziness quotient to play on the cop's sympathies.

He'd reached the rear of the BMW when she thought of a quite obvious problem she'd overlooked. Two of them, actually. The car she was driving was not hers. The person it belonged to was dead, a smoldering pile of ashes now in her picturesque backyard. Providing Amelia had been telling the truth about where her husband and children were, it was unlikely the BMW had been reported stolen. Except it didn't matter because the cop would want to see Noreen's license, which would identify her as a fugitive.

Goddammit.

She wanted to scream.

Everything was going wrong and she was fucking sick of it.

She looked at the side-view mirror and saw the cop was within just a few feet of her open window.

Fuck this.

Noreen summoned every ounce of blood-amplified strength at her command and threw the door open, launching herself out of the car with a speed and force no human being could hope to match. The cop was just starting to pull his weapon when Noreen wrapped herself around him and crushed him against the side of the BMW, bending his head backward over the low roof as her fangs tore into his throat. Several cars sped by as she drank the man's blood. One driver honked, but it was nearly dark now and she thought it unlikely anyone could tell exactly what was happening.

The cop sagged beneath her, his hand falling away from his gun as his arm went limp. He was fading, spiraling away toward unconsciousness, but she was able to walk him back over to the cruiser and drop him back in behind the wheel. As she did this, she was aware she was probably being recorded by both the officer's body cam and the vehicle's dash cam, but Noreen didn't care. She cared only about buying just enough time to get away.

She slammed the cruiser's door shut and leaned in through the open window just long enough to rip open a bigger wound in the man's throat. A great gout of blood leaped from the wound and splashed against the dash.

Moments later, Noreen was back behind the wheel of the BMW and driving away.

Five minutes after that, the exit to Stillwater Lake came into view.

She put her blinker on.

Her kids were up there at the cabin.

She knew it, could feel it in her blood.

A smile curved her blood-smeared face.

She couldn't wait to see them again.

TWENTY-EIGHT

SOMETHING IN THE ASSURED WAY the stranger carried himself triggered an inclination within Zach to afford him the same deference he would show a policeman or other authority figure. For about a fraction of a second there, he might have turned his gun over to the man had he demanded it. This was the lingering influence of lessons instilled in him since childhood, but the mental reflex wasn't powerful enough to make Zach drop his guard. They'd been through too much today for that.

Instead of lowering the gun, he tightened his grip on it and aimed the muzzle squarely at the center of the man's face. "We don't know you. Why should we talk to you about anything?"

The man who'd called himself Mr. McCabe gave a slight, almost imperceptible smile. "Because you're confused and scared. Because you've been backed into a corner with no obvious way out. You don't even really know what's going on." He spread his hands in front of him and shrugged. "Aren't you ready to get some answers to your questions? You've been through a lot. I can see it in your faces. You must be so very tired. Aren't you ready for some help?"

The way the man said these things made it all sound so sensible. His tone carried a reassuring quality of wisdom, the kind earned only through experience. Listening to him, Zach felt a deep yearning, a wish to turn all this trouble over to a grownup who knew what he was doing. It was similar to how he used to feel when taking a problem he couldn't solve to his father. Once again, he had to remind himself he didn't know this man and therefore couldn't know if he was truly worthy of trust. He might yet turn out to be an enemy.

McCabe nodded, smiling again. "You don't know if you can trust me."

Zach and his sister exchanged a look but said nothing.

McCabe grunted. "Of course you don't. It's perfectly understandable. You've never set eyes on me before and don't know me from Adam, but I will tell you this in the hope that you take it to heart. Your situation is even more dire than you already know."

Zach's laughter then came with a spark of derision. "Mister, I'm sure you believe that, but you might feel differently if you'd gone through what we just went through here. Because I gotta tell you, I'm kind of having a hard time imagining anything more fucking dire than that."

McCabe's gaze went to the bullet-riddled front door, lingering there for a moment before again settling on the siblings. "Perhaps you should explain, but I'd caution you to be concise. There are important things I need to tell you and preparations must be made, but we don't have a lot of time."

Zach glanced at Chelsea. "You want to tell him, or should I?"

She shrugged. "You go ahead, but he's right. Be quick about it so we can get out of here."

Zach heeded her advice as he delivered a condensed account of what they'd experienced at the cabin since their arrival, hitting all the major highlights without going into elaborate detail.

McCabe's unwavering attention was on him the entire time he spoke, the look on his face thoughtful and empathetic. He cleared his throat when Zach fell silent. "These coffins you spoke of are around the back?"

Zach nodded. "Yeah."

McCabe gave another of his little smiles. "I won't diminish what you've experienced as I know it was terrifying, as well as painful." He glanced at Chelsea, clearly directing that last bit at her. "But this is actually a problem with a simple solution. Give me just a moment."

He turned away from them and approached the Mercedes, a beep sounding when he pressed a button on his key fob, causing the vehicle's trunk to pop open. At the rear of the car, he lifted the lid up and leaned into the trunk, disappearing from view for a moment. They heard grumbling noises as he moved some things around. Then he stood up straight again and slammed the lid shut, approaching the cabin with a large white plastic jug.

Zach frowned. "What the hell is that?"

McCabe didn't break stride as he glanced at Zach and veered toward the side of the cabin. "Follow me and see for yourselves."

After a brief hesitation, Zach and Chelsea stepped down from the porch and trailed after McCabe as he moved hurriedly along the side of the cabin and emerged into the parking area in back. He continued in a straight line toward the shed, again not breaking stride or showing signs of fear.

Zach had difficulty believing a force as powerful as the one that had tormented them could be countered as easily as McCabe claimed, but the man's obvious high level of confidence stirred a flicker of hope anyway. If what he was saying proved true, that instinct to defer to his unspoken authority might become harder to resist.

The instant he arrived at the shed, McCabe screwed the cap off the big white jug and began pouring out a thick line of a glistening white substance along the front of the structure.

Zach moved in for a closer look. "Is that . . . salt?"

McCabe grunted in affirmation. "It is indeed, but please stay back. The binding circle must not be broken."

As instructed, Zach ventured no closer to the trail of salt, but he and his sister followed along with McCabe as the man continued to pour out a thick line of the substance around the entire shed. "Are you being for real with this? Is it supposed to be like in TV shows and movies where you trap demons and ghosts this way?"

McCabe chuckled. "It's exactly like that, young man. You'd be surprised how many of the hoary old tropes portrayed in popular works of fiction are rooted firmly in actual occult practice." He ceased pouring the line of salt as they returned to the front of the shed, after completing the unbroken trail. "This is merely a temporary solution. Things will start happening fast soon enough and you'll both need to be stronger and braver than you've already been in order to survive. Once all that's over, I'll fetch a can of gasoline from my car and set the shed ablaze. By reducing the creatures in those coffins to ash, we'll end the problem in a more permanent way."

Zach frowned. "Creatures? What kind of creatures?"

McCabe looked to the woods beyond the shed, scowling at the

dark line of trees for a moment before saying. "Night has fallen. We should continue this discussion inside."

Zach heaved an exasperated sigh and looked at Chelsea.

She looked at McCabe, her expression open and hopeful, ready to believe in this man they'd just met not even fifteen minutes ago. "It's really safe to go back in? Because I was thinking it'd be better if we just left this place."

He nodded, smiling again. "It really is. As safe as it can be anyway. And the time for running away has passed. Trust me when I say this is where we all need to be at this point in time. A moment of reckoning is nearly at hand. Once that reckoning has occurred, the worst of your problems will be over."

The notion of the worst of their problems being resolved appealed to Zach, but the rest of McCabe's words struck him as both cryptic and ominous. He opened his mouth to voice this sentiment, but by then the man was already moving toward the cabin.

Zach and Chelsea followed.

What else was there to do?

This man claimed to have the answers to all their questions. There'd been no more mental intrusions from the mysterious force since his arrival. At this point, refusing to hear him out seemed unwise.

Barely more than a minute later, the three of them were inside the cabin, standing in the main room with the bullet-riddled door closed and locked again.

McCabe looked at each of them in turn before speaking, holding their gazes for several seconds at a time, appearing to need a moment to gauge something within them before beginning.

Then he nodded and said, "Right. Well, here it is. Your parents are vampires."

Zach and his sister looked at each other. If anyone had uttered those words just a day earlier, each of them would have instantly burst out laughing, but not now. He could tell from the look on Chelsea's face they were thinking of the same thing, the refrigerator in the storage unit filled with blood bags. The additional blood bags right here in the cabin. The black coffins they'd encountered today at multiple locations associated with their parents. These factors and many more rendered the concept anything but amusing.

Chelsea frowned. "But they walk around in daylight. They eat regular food, drink alcohol, do all kinds of regular human shit."

McCabe nodded again, his smile one of indulgence. "That's because they're daywalkers. There are multiple species of vampires. Your parents happen to be the kind most capable of passing for normal people. There's another species called nightsiders, and they more closely resemble the creatures you know from fiction. But make no mistake, each species is just as deadly."

Zach groaned, a sound of weariness rather than skepticism. "This is the part where we're supposed to be thick-headed and tell you how crazy that sounds, but the really crazy thing is I believe you. One-hundred percent."

Chelsea sighed. "I guess I do too. When you decide to let yourself believe blood-sucking creatures of the night are real, suddenly all the shit that was so hard to understand starts making sense."

McCabe nodded steadily as he listened to this exchange. "Yes, I imagine that's true, and believe me, it pains me to have to tell you these things. These are the people who raised you. Your whole lives have revolved around them. Even now, in the midst of your confusion and resentment, you surely still harbor love for them. It is only natural. But trust me when I tell you that you must find it within yourselves to push beyond those base emotions and see the ugliest part of this truth. Your parents are supernatural predators. They are remorseless killers. Many innocent people have died at their hands over a long period of time. You must therefore stand against them alongside me."

The onset of a headache caused Zach to rub at his forehead as he listened to McCabe speak. He didn't fully know yet what the man expected of them, but he sensed it was something that would be immensely difficult in more ways than one.

"Okay, look, you're telling us some pretty hardcore, fucked up shit about our mom and dad, and yeah, there's some evidence to support some of it, but I still don't get how they had time for all this killing. How would they have done it without us knowing? Without having even the tiniest hint? It seems almost impossible."

McCabe made a noise of sympathy, but his face became pinched in a way that suggested a declining level of patience. "I'll explain what I can. Please understand that some of this is informed conjecture rather than firsthand knowledge. As you know, until very recently, your parents were under the radar, well-hidden from hunters as well as the vampire world itself. It wasn't until your father's friend tipped us off that the carefully crafted facade began to fall apart. We didn't know until this very day that your mother was also a vampire. Once that fact came to light, I began to suspect that Noreen and Jonathan Murphy might actually be two of the most notorious fugitives known to vampire society."

Zach did a double take at this statement. "Say what the fuck?"

McCabe smiled. "Not only are your parents vampires, they are brazen criminals. It would not be inaccurate to call them the Bonnie and Clyde of the vampire underworld. Many years ago, beginning in the mid '70s, they embarked on a series of daring robberies and heists, always targeting the most powerful and richest vampires. The elder vampires, the richest ones, tend to hoard their wealth in hard currency, keeping it with them at all times. Banks, of course, become problematic for creatures that live for centuries. It's understandable, but it created a vulnerability your parents exploited. They would go in with overwhelming force, guns blazing, often utilizing expendable teams of hired mercenaries. By the time they went underground for good, they'd amassed a cash fortune of countless millions."

The siblings gaped at him in open-mouthed amazement.

Then Zach swallowed a lump in his throat and said, "Holy shit. And you know all this for a fact?"

McCabe shook his head. "In fact, I don't. It is, as I've said, conjecture, but of a highly informed variety. I've been in the creature hunting business for a long time. Those of us who do this in a dedicated, professional way are all familiar with the exploits of your parents, which are legendary. Based on information you've provided, in addition to other evidence, it is my highly educated guess that your parents are indeed this notorious duo. I am frankly astonished they've managed to successfully remain at large for this long. The generally held view has long been that they were secretly apprehended and killed many years ago. News of their survival would send shockwaves through vampiric circles. In human society, it'd be equivalent to discovering conclusive proof of D.B. Cooper's true identity."

Chelsea looked askance at him. "D.B. who?"

McCabe said, "A man who hijacked a plane a long time ago and parachuted into a driving rainstorm with a briefcase full of money. He called himself D.B. Cooper. It wasn't his real name. He was never found."

Zach's mind reeled at the string of dizzying revelations. He eyed the weapons piled up on the round table and thought about all the other things they'd found in the storage unit. The fridge full of blood was pretty damning, but so were the mountains of cash. Taken together, it all gave McCabe's story a hell of a lot of credence. That bit about his parents' purported crime spree starting in the '70s gave him pause for a moment, but it also fit with the entire premise of them being vampires.

His eyes sharpened as his gaze returned to McCabe. "How did you find this place if you didn't start putting all this together until today? Mom told us they bought it under another fake identity."

McCabe nodded. "That's correct. I did not personally unearth the information. The credit for that goes to a skilled hacker whose services I sometimes engage. It's true that your parents were well-hidden. They might have remained so indefinitely if not for some of Jonathan Murphy's recent indiscretions, beginning when he made the mistake of confiding in a friend. That first crack in the facade was all the young lady in my employ needed to start unraveling all of it, though it took most of the day. The truth is I didn't know this place existed until little more than an hour ago. I was tracking your mother on the road when she stopped at a rest area. While she was inside, presumably availing herself of the facilities, I received the call telling me all I needed to know. I left ahead of her in hopes of reaching you first."

Zach frowned. "This hacker girl, she told you we were here?"

McCabe shook his head. "That was another educated guess. Now then, do you feel you are sufficiently informed? Because we need to talk about what we're going to do when your mother arrives."

Zach made a contemplative sound as he slowly nodded. "Uh-huh. And what would that be?"

McCabe's expression turned grim. "She must be killed, of course. She is a mass-murdering fiend who has long eluded justice."

Zach grunted. "Yeah, I should've figured you'd say something like that. I get that she's done bad things, our dad too, but do you really expect us to help you kill either of them? They're our flesh and blood."

Chelsea nodded in an adamant way. "I agree with my brother. Maybe Mom should face some kind of justice, I don't know. Maybe everything you're saying is right." Sudden tears welled in her eyes and she wiped them away as they began to slide down her cheeks. "But she's our *mother*."

The extra emphasis she gave that last word was something Zach felt on a gut level. "Look, I don't know what's right here. We might not keep you from doing whatever it is you think you have to do, but we're not helping."

For the first time since the man's arrival at the cabin, there was a detectable spark of anger in his expression. "This talk of loyalty to flesh and blood is all very heartwarming, but you should know that in all likelihood you are not the flesh and blood offspring of the vampires who raised you. You are also quite likely not actually brother and sister, at least in the biological sense."

These pronouncements elicited audible gasps from Zach and Chelsea.

Chelsea shook her head. "No. I don't believe that. It can't be."

McCabe smirked. "Oh, but it can be, because while it's true that of all the vampiric species, daywalkers are the most biologically compatible with humans, daywalker females are not capable of giving birth. I can't tell you who your real parents are, but I can almost guarantee that when you were both very young, perhaps even when you were only infants, you were stolen from them. These despicable creatures then raised you as their own, not out of love, but as part of their insidious scheme to fit in with normal human society. You should despise them both for the scourge that they are, burn with a relentless yearning to wipe them off the face of the earth."

Zach's head felt like it was spinning again, and judging from the look on her face, Chelsea felt the same way. They'd already been asked to process an overload of shocking information in a short amount of time, but this latest allegation from McCabe felt like a step too far.

He moved a few steps farther away from the man, shaking his head repeatedly in abject denial. "No. No. Fuck that. And even if you're right, fuck it anyway. I grew up with her." He indicated his sister with an emphatic head gesture. "Blood or not, she is my sister."

Chelsea sneered at McCabe. "Fuck yes, I am. And he's my brother, now and forever. Tell me something, Mr. Vampire Hunter. Were you in charge of hiring the one-eyed piece of shit you sent to our house? Hmm? What would you think if I told you he molested me when he had me alone? What does it say about you that you'd send that kind of animal after us?"

McCabe looked rattled for a moment, flinching as she revealed this information, but he quickly recovered. "What it tells me," he said, sighing as he straightened his tie, "is that the business I am in is a hard and merciless one, and sometimes one must hire hard and merciless men to get things done. What happened to you is unfortunate, but it is part of the risk inherent in so frequently dealing with these unsavory types."

Zach scowled. "The end justifies the means, that's basically what you're saying?"

McCabe lifted his chin, affecting an air of stalwart dignity. "In this business, that is always the case. In any event, the matter is not up for debate. I will do what is necessary when your mother arrives, and you *will* help me."

Zach's scowl deepened.

Had he really thought this man had all the answers?

He was an arrogant piece of shit.

Anger roiled inside Zach for another few moments before his scowl slowly softened, yielding to a smile as he raised his gun and aimed it at the hunter's head. The man's look of surprised, wide-eyed alarm almost made him laugh. McCabe's mouth opened as he sputtered half-formed words that added up to nothing.

He was still struggling to compose himself when everyone in the room was distracted by the metallic click of a key turning in the lock of the cabin's front door. Three sets of eyes moved in that direction at the same time, followed by multiple gasps as the door swung inward, revealing a grinning Noreen Murphy standing just outside the doorway. She was wearing a short black dress her kids had never seen her in before. The dress was a bloody mess, and her face was smeared with crimson.

"Mom," Chelsea gasped in a soft voice, her eyes shimmering again.

"Hello, baby," Noreen told her, still grinning as she stepped through the open doorway into the cabin. Then her gaze went to Zach as she eyed the weapon gripped in his hand. "My son, I'm so proud of you, seeing through this man's bullshit and standing up for yourself this way. For your sister too. I've been listening at the door for a while, and you are both amazing."

McCabe started fumbling for something in a pocket of his trench coat.

"Stop that," Zach told him.

McCabe ignored him, shoving his hand deep inside the pocket. It came out again an instant later, gripping a large wooden stake. He raised it high in the air over his shoulder, hand shaking as he addressed their mother. "Stay back! I'm warning you. I'll end you now if you come one step closer."

Noreen tossed her head back and laughed heartily. "No, you won't, you silly man. An actual fucking stake? Are you serious? What kind of cosplay nonsense is this?" She laughed some more, looking again at her son. "I could end this man in the blink of an eye, sweetheart. I'd do it so fast he'd never even see me move. But I think this moment should belong to you. Do you know what I think you should do?"

McCabe trembled as he looked back and forth between them, sweat pouring from his brow, but Zach ignored him, focusing on his mother. He watched her eyes, studied her features, looking for signs of being manipulated in some cynical way. All he saw was the pride she'd claimed.

He let out a breath, steadying his grip on the gun. "Why don't you tell me, Mom?"

She smiled sweetly. "I think you should kill the hunter, Zach."

A creak of floorboards from the back of the cabin caused everyone to look in that direction, and what Zach saw as his head turned unleashed a tidal wave of conflicting emotions within him. Anger and bitter resentment, as well as a sense of shock so intense it nearly knocked him off his feet, but also a feeling of great relief and joy.

Chelsea sniffled. "Daddy."

Jonathan Murphy was smiling as he came out of the kitchen into the main room. "Hi, sweetheart," he told his daughter before focusing on his son. "I agree with your mother, bud. Kill the hunter."

Zach looked at his sister.

Chelsea nodded her encouragement. "Kill him, Zach. Be the hero. Kill the fucking hunter."

McCabe screeched in terror, raising the stake higher as he ran at Noreen.

Zach felt the gun jerk in his hand as he squeezed the trigger, but his aim was true, delivering a bullet to the crown of McCabe's skull. It blew the man's forehead apart on the way out, but kept going in an altered trajectory, spinning and nicking Noreen's shoulder. She caught the falling corpse in her arms and clamped her mouth to the gushing exit wound.

Some noisy slurping sounds ensued.

They went on for a while.

TWENTY-NINE

THE REUNION WITH HER LONG-absent husband occurred not long after Noreen ditched the BMW near the bottom of the long private drive. After pulling in just far enough to leave the vehicle parked out of the view of anyone passing by on the road, she got out and started walking up the drive to the cabin. She did this because she wasn't sure what the situation there would be when she arrived, and a stealthy approach sans engine noise seemed the best way to go.

She sensed Jonathan's presence before she saw him, feeling it like a uniquely identifiable shift in the atmosphere. They'd been the most intimate of partners for almost fifty years prior to his disappearance. It would've been impossible for him to hide when he was this nearby.

"You might as well come out," she told him, stopping in the middle of the narrow strip of asphalt. "Hiding time is over."

He needed no further prompting, coming out of the woods and approaching her with that familiar roguish smile on his handsome face. The most interesting thing to her in that first moment was that he appeared nicely groomed and his clothes were clean. It was not the look of a man who'd been lying low in the wilderness for a protracted time.

They faced each other in the middle of the lane, separated by only a few feet.

"I imagine you probably want to kill me," he told her.

She nodded. "I've wanted to for a long while now. I've dreamed of it. Fantasized about the ways I'd torture you before ending you forever, how I'd draw it out for weeks, maybe months, before finishing it."

He shrugged. "I did a bad thing. A selfish thing. And we both know it doesn't end there. I won't give you excuses. You'd be justified in taking your vengeance. Our kids are up at the cabin."

Noreen sighed. "I thought as much."

Jonathan's features sharpened, conveying curiosity. "Why would they have come here unaccompanied?"

"It's been a long and difficult day."

She gave him an abbreviated account of events.

"Huh. Well. They showed up a few hours ago. I took off into the woods when I heard them coming. The car I've been using is at another cabin, so they never knew I was in the area. There's a dangerous man up there with them now. A human. A hunter."

She frowned. "A hunter? Are you sure?"

"Pretty sure. He has that look. Smug and self-righteous. Also, he poured a salt circle around the shed in back."

Noreen felt her blood beginning to boil. She could well imagine the things a man like that would be telling her children. He had no right, even if many of those things were true. "The elders must have been stirring."

Jonathan nodded. "Yes, I think so. They're dangerous despite the steps we've taken to neutralize their powers. We've been too complacent where they're concerned, keeping them for so long. They might yet grow strong enough in their slumber to escape and come after us."

"What should we do?"

"The only thing we can do. We have to destroy them."

Noreen grunted. "I suppose that would be for the best. We've gotten all the use from them we ever will."

Jonathan smiled, clearly pleased she saw things his way, at least in this one matter. "Exactly."

They stared at each other in silence for a moment.

Then Jonathan said, "So what now?"

"What else? Let's go see our kids. Any other business between you and me can wait."

So they walked up to the cabin together, Jonathan going around to the back while Noreen walked right up to the front door. She'd envisioned a violent confrontation between herself and the hunter, possibly with some involvement from her husband. That changed as she stood there at the front door and listened to the conversation taking place inside the cabin. She felt herself swell with pride as her kids stood up to the hunter, defying him and calling him out for his own transgressions. It wasn't long before she realized the situation had only one resolution that might result in the kids still wanting a relationship with her.

They had to be the ones to put an end to it all.

She was so grateful Jonathan had clearly sensed the same thing.

The questions from the kids began almost as soon as the hunter was dead on the floor. How much of what the man had told them about their outlaw past was true? Were they really vampires? Did they really need to drink human blood every day to survive? What did all this mean for the future of this family?

But that wasn't all.

Information was demanded from their father about where he'd been and what he'd been doing all that time he was gone. He was transparent with them, attributing his actions to his own selfish needs. He never actually apologized, but he did say he was ready to be with his family again if they would have him.

There was some discussion on the matter after that, but not much. Not so deep down, it was what they all wanted anyway, even if there were a few minor misgivings here and there.

After arriving at this more or less happy conclusion, Zach asked his father a version of the same question the man had asked his wife a short while ago. "So what do we do now? We can't go home again."

Jonathan and Noreen exchanged a long look of silent communication, their thoughts as clear to each other as spoken words.

Then Jonathan smiled at his kids. "How does everyone feel about a long road trip? We can go anywhere in the country. Anywhere in the world. Seriously. We have the resources to do any damn thing we want. It's up to you."

The road trip idea was greeted with great enthusiasm.

A short while later, after taking care of some loose ends around the cabin, they piled into the dead hunter's Mercedes and drove away.

Behind them, tongues of flame stretched to the sky as the shed and its long-slumbering inhabitants burned.

BIO

Bryan Smith is the author of numerous novels and novellas, including *Depraved, 68 Kill, The Unseen, Slowly We Rot, Dead End House, Last of the Ravagers,* and *Kill for Satan!,* which won a Splatterpunk Award for best horror novella of 2018. He won a second Splatterpunk Award in 2020 for *Dirty Rotten Hippies and Other Stories.* He is also the co-author of *Suburban Gothic,* written with Brian Keene. A film version of *68 Kill* was released in 2017. He lives in TN with his dog Mac. Signed copies of his books can be purchased at bryansmithhorror.bigcartel.com

Spotify playlist for Kill the Hunter:
https://open.spotify.com/playlist/3fQCMS2qcpSW9C3GcJdMTi?s
i=430ab2ba54494b05

Other Grindhouse Press Titles